The Circle

A Comedy in Three Acts

&

East of Suez

A Play in Seven Scenes

W. Somerset Maugham

The Circle: A Comedy in Three Acts & East of Suez: A Play in Seven Scenes

ISBN: 978-1-61895-979-9

CONTENT

THE CIRCLE

EAST OF SUEZ

THE CIRCLE

PERSONS OF THE PLAY

Clive Champion-Cheney
Arnold Champion-Cheney, M.P.
Lord Porteous
Edward Luton
Lady Catherine Champion-Cheney
Elizabeth
Mrs. Shenstone.

The action takes place at Aston-Adey, Arnold Champion-Cheney's house in Dorset.

THE FIRST ACT

The Scene is a stately drawing-room at Aston-Adey, with fine pictures on the walls and Georgian furniture. Aston-Adey has been described, with many illustrations, in Country Life. It is not a house, but a place. Its owner takes a great pride in it, and there is nothing in the room which is not of the period. Through the French windows at the back can be seen the beautiful gardens which are one of the features.

It is a fine summer morning.

Arnold comes in. He is a man of about thirty-five, tall and good-looking, fair, with a clean-cut, sensitive face. He has a look that is intellectual, but somewhat bloodless. He is very well dressed.

Arnold. [*Calling.*] Elizabeth! [*He goes to the window and calls again.*] Elizabeth! [*He rings the bell. While he is waiting he gives a look round the room. He slightly alters the position of one of the chairs. He takes an ornament from the chimney-piece and blows the dust from it.*]

[*A Footman comes in.*]

Oh, George! see if you can find Mrs. Cheney, and ask her if she'd be good enough to come here.

Footman. Very good, sir.

[*The Footman turns to go.*]

Arnold. Who is supposed to look after this room?

Footman. I don't know, sir.

Arnold. I wish when they dust they'd take care to replace the things exactly as they were before.

Footman. Yes, sir.

Arnold. [*Dismissing him.*] All right.

[*The Footman goes out. He goes again to the window and calls.*]

Arnold. Elizabeth! [*He sees Mrs. Shenstone.*] Oh, Anna, do you know where Elizabeth is?

2

[*Mrs. Shenstone comes in from the garden. She is a woman of forty, pleasant and of elegant appearance.*]

Anna. Isn't she playing tennis?

Arnold. No, I've been down to the tennis court. Something very tiresome has happened.

Anna. Oh?

Arnold. I wonder where the deuce she is.

Anna. When do you expect Lord Porteous and Lady Kitty?

Arnold. They're motoring down in time for luncheon.

Anna. Are you sure you want me to be here? It's not too late yet, you know. I can have my things packed and catch a train for somewhere or other.

Arnold. No, of course we want you. It'll make it so much easier if there are people here. It was exceedingly kind of you to come.

Anna. Oh, nonsense!

Arnold. And I think it was a good thing to have Teddie Luton down.

Anna. He is so breezy, isn't he?

Arnold. Yes, that's his great asset. I don't know that he's very intelligent, but, you know, there are occasions when you want a bull in a china shop. I sent one of the servants to find Elizabeth.

Anna. I daresay she's putting on her shoes. She and Teddie were going to have a single.

Arnold. It can't take all this time to change one's shoes.

Anna. [*With a smile.*] One can't change one's shoes without powdering one's nose, you know.

[*Elizabeth comes in. She is a very pretty creature in the early twenties. She wears a light summer frock.*]

Arnold. My dear, I've been hunting for you everywhere. What *have* you been doing?

Elizabeth. Nothing! I've been standing on my head.

Arnold. My father's here.

Elizabeth. [*Startled.*] Where?

Arnold. At the cottage. He arrived last night.

Elizabeth. Damn!

Arnold. [*Good-humouredly.*] I wish you wouldn't say that, Elizabeth.

Elizabeth. If you're not going to say "Damn" when a thing's damnable, when are you going to say "Damn"?

Arnold. I should have thought you could say, "Oh, bother!" or something like that.

3

Elizabeth. But that wouldn't express my sentiments. Besides, at that speech day when you were giving away the prizes you said there were no synonyms in the English language.

Anna. [*Smiling.*] Oh, Elizabeth! it's very unfair to expect a politician to live in private up to the statements he makes in public.

Arnold. I'm always willing to stand by anything I've said. There *are* no synonyms in the English language.

Elizabeth. In that case I shall be regretfully forced to continue to say "Damn" whenever I feel like it.

[*Edward Luton shows himself at the window. He is an attractive youth in flannels.*]

Teddie. I say, what about this tennis?

Elizabeth. Come in. We're having a scene.

Teddie. [*Entering.*] How splendid! What about?

Elizabeth. The English language.

Teddie. Don't tell me you've been splitting your infinitives.

Arnold. [*With the shadow of a frown.*] I wish you'd be serious, Elizabeth. The situation is none too pleasant.

Anna. I think Teddie and I had better make ourselves scarce.

Elizabeth. Nonsense! You're both in it. If there's going to be any unpleasantness we want your moral support. That's why we asked you to come.

Teddie. And I thought I'd been asked for my blue eyes.

Elizabeth. Vain beast! And they happen to be brown.

Teddie. Is anything up?

Elizabeth. Arnold's father arrived last night.

Teddie. Did he, by Jove! I thought he was in Paris.

Arnold. So did we all. He told me he'd be there for the next month.

Anna. Have you seen him?

Arnold. No! he rang me up. It's a mercy he had a telephone put in the cottage. It would have been a pretty kettle of fish if he'd just walked in.

Elizabeth. Did you tell him Lady Catherine was coming?

Arnold. Of course not. I was flabbergasted to know he was here. And then I thought we'd better talk it over first.

Elizabeth. Is he coming along here?

Arnold. Yes. He suggested it, and I couldn't think of any excuse to prevent him.

Teddie. Couldn't you put the other people off?

Arnold. They're coming by car. They may be here any minute. It's too late to do that.

4

Elizabeth. Besides, it would be beastly.

Arnold. I knew it was silly to have them here. Elizabeth insisted.

Elizabeth. After all, she *is* your mother, Arnold.

Arnold. That meant precious little to her when she—went away. You can't imagine it means very much to me now.

Elizabeth. It's thirty years ago. It seems so absurd to bear malice after all that time.

Arnold. I don't bear malice, but the fact remains that she did me the most irreparable harm. I can find no excuse for her.

Elizabeth. Have you ever tried to?

Arnold. My dear Elizabeth, it's no good going over all that again. The facts are lamentably simple. She had a husband who adored her, a wonderful position, all the money she could want, and a child of five. And she ran away with a married man.

Elizabeth. Lady Porteous is not a very attractive woman, Arnold. [*To Anna.*] Do you know her?

Anna. [*Smiling.*] "Forbidding" is the word, I think.

Arnold. If you're going to make little jokes about it, I have nothing more to say.

Anna. I'm sorry, Arnold.

Elizabeth. Perhaps your mother couldn't help herself—if she was in love?

Arnold. And had no sense of honour, duty, or decency? Oh, yes, under those circumstances you can explain a great deal.

Elizabeth. That's not a very pretty way to speak of your mother.

Arnold. I can't look on her as my mother.

Elizabeth. What you can't get over is that she didn't think of you. Some of us are more mother and some of us more woman. It gives me a little thrill when I think that she loved that man so much. She sacrificed her name, her position, and her child to him.

Arnold. You really can't expect the said child to have any great affection for the mother who treated him like that.

Elizabeth. No, I don't think I do. But I think it's a pity after all these years that you shouldn't be friends.

Arnold. I wonder if you realise what it was to grow up under the shadow of that horrible scandal. Everywhere, at school, and at Oxford, and afterwards in London, I was always the son of Lady Kitty Cheney. Oh, it was cruel, cruel!

Elizabeth. Yes, I know, Arnold. It was beastly for you.

Arnold. It would have been bad enough if it had been an ordinary case, but the position of the people made it ten times worse. My father was in the House then, and Porteous—he hadn't

5

succeeded to the title—was in the House too; he was Under-Secretary for Foreign Affairs, and he was very much in the public eye.

Anna. My father always used to say he was the ablest man in the party. Every one was expecting him to be Prime Minister.

Arnold. You can imagine what a boon it was to the British public. They hadn't had such a treat for a generation. The most popular song of the day was about my mother. Did you ever hear it? "Naughty Lady Kitty. Thought it such a pity . . ."

Elizabeth. [*Interrupting.*] Oh, Arnold, don't!

Arnold. And then they never let people forget them. If they'd lived quietly in Florence and not made a fuss the scandal would have died down. But those constant actions between Lord and Lady Porteous kept on reminding everyone.

Teddie. What were they having actions about?

Arnold. Of course my father divorced his wife, but Lady Porteous refused to divorce Porteous. He tried to force her by refusing to support her and turning her out of her house, and heaven knows what. They were constantly wrangling in the law courts.

Anna. I think it was monstrous of Lady Porteous.

Arnold. She knew he wanted to marry my mother, and she hated my mother. You can't blame her.

Anna. It must have been very difficult for them.

Arnold. That's why they've lived in Florence. Porteous has money. They found people there who were willing to accept the situation.

Elizabeth. This is the first time they've ever come to England.

Arnold. My father will have to be told, Elizabeth.

Elizabeth. Yes.

Anna. [*To Elizabeth.*] Has he ever spoken to you about Lady Kitty?

Elizabeth. Never.

Arnold. I don't think her name has passed his lips since she ran away from this house thirty years ago.

Teddie. Oh, they lived here?

Arnold. Naturally. There was a house-party, and one evening neither Porteous nor my mother came down to dinner. The rest of them waited. They couldn't make it out. My father sent up to my mother's room, and a note was found on the pincushion.

Elizabeth. [*With a faint smile.*] That's what they did in the Dark Ages.

Arnold. I think he took a dislike to this house from that horrible night. He never lived here again, and when I married he

6

handed the place over to me. He just has a cottage now on the estate that he comes to when he feels inclined.

Elizabeth. It's been very nice for us.

Arnold. I owe everything to my father. I don't think he'll ever forgive me for asking these people to come here.

Elizabeth. I'm going to take all the blame on myself, Arnold.

Arnold. [*Irritably.*] The situation was embarrassing enough anyhow. I don't know how I ought to treat them.

Elizabeth. Don't you think that'll settle itself when you see them?

Arnold. After all, they're my guests. I shall try and behave like a gentleman.

Elizabeth. I wouldn't. We haven't got central heating.

Arnold. [*Taking no notice.*] Will she expect me to kiss her?

Elizabeth. [*With a smile.*] Surely.

Arnold. It always makes me uncomfortable when people are effusive.

Anna. But I can't understand why you never saw her before.

Arnold. I believe she tried to see me when I was little, but my father thought it better she shouldn't.

Anna. Yes, but when you were grown up?

Arnold. She was always in Italy. I never went to Italy.

Elizabeth. It seems to me so pathetic that if you saw one another in the street you wouldn't recognise each other.

Arnold. Is it my fault?

Elizabeth. You've promised to be very gentle with her and very kind.

Arnold. The mistake was asking Porteous to come too. It looks as though we condoned the whole thing. And how am I to treat him? Am I to shake him by the hand and slap him on the back? He absolutely ruined my father's life.

Elizabeth. [*Smiling.*] How much would you give for a nice motor accident that prevented them from coming?

Arnold. I let you persuade me against my better judgment, and I've regretted it ever since.

Elizabeth. [*Good-humouredly.*] I think it's very lucky that Anna and Teddie are here. I don't foresee a very successful party.

Arnold. I'm going to do my best. I gave you my promise and I shall keep it. But I can't answer for my father.

Anna. Here is your father.

[*Mr. Champion-Cheney shows himself at one of the French windows.*]

C.-C. May I come in through the window, or shall I have myself announced by a supercilious flunkey?

Elizabeth. Come in. We've been expecting you.

C.-C. Impatiently, I hope, my dear child.

[*Mr. Champion-Cheney is a tall man in the early sixties, spare, with a fine head of gray hair and an intelligent, somewhat ascetic face. He is very carefully dressed. He is a man who makes the most of himself. He bears his years jauntily. He kisses Elizabeth and then holds out his hand to Arnold.*]

Elizabeth. We thought you'd be in Paris for another month.

C.-C. How are you, Arnold? I always reserve to myself the privilege of changing my mind. It's the only one elderly gentlemen share with pretty women.

Elizabeth. You know Anna.

C.-C. [*Shaking hands with her.*] Of course I do. How very nice to see you here! Are you staying long?

Anna. As long as I'm welcome.

Elizabeth. And this is Mr. Luton.

C.-C. How do you do? Do you play bridge?

Luton. I do.

C.-C. Capital. Do you declare without top honours?

Luton. Never.

C.-C. Of such is the kingdom of heaven. I see that you are a good young man.

Luton. But, like the good in general, I am poor.

C.-C. Never mind; if your principles are right, you can play ten shillings a hundred without danger. I never play less, and I never play more.

Arnold. And you—are you going to stay long, father?

C.-C. To luncheon, if you'll have me.

[*Arnold gives Elizabeth a harassed look.*]

Elizabeth. That'll be jolly.

Arnold. I didn't mean that. Of course you're going to stay for luncheon. I meant, how long are you going to stay down here?

C.-C. A week.

[*There is a moment's pause. Everyone but Champion-Cheney is slightly embarrassed.*]

Teddie. I think we'd better chuck our tennis.

Elizabeth. Yes. I want my father-in-law to tell me what they're wearing in Paris this week.

Teddie. I'll go and put the rackets away.

[*Teddie goes out.*]

Arnold. It's nearly one o'clock, Elizabeth.

Elizabeth. I didn't know it was so late.

Anna. [*To Arnold.*] I wonder if I can persuade you to take a turn in the garden before luncheon.

Arnold. [*Jumping at the idea.*] I'd love it.

[*Anna goes out of the window, and as he follows her he stops irresolutely.*]

I want you to look at this chair I've just got. I think it's rather good.

C.-C. Charming.

Arnold. About 1750, I should say. Good design, isn't it? It hasn't been restored or anything.

C.-C. Very pretty.

Arnold. I think it was a good buy, don't you?

C.-C. Oh, my dear boy! you know I'm entirely ignorant about these things.

Arnold. It's exactly my period . . . I shall see you at luncheon, then.

[*He follows Anna through the window.*]

C.-C. Who is that young man?

Elizabeth. Mr. Luton. He's only just been demobilised. He's the manager of a rubber estate in the F.M.S.

C.-C. And what are the F.M.S. when they're at home?

Elizabeth. The Federated Malay States. He joined up at the beginning of the war. He's just going back there.

Elizabeth. Have we? I didn't notice it.

C.-C. I suppose it's difficult for the young to realise that one may be old without being a fool.

Elizabeth. I never thought you that. Everyone knows you're very intelligent.

C.-C. They certainly ought to by now. I've told them often enough. Are you a little nervous?

Elizabeth. Let me feel my pulse. [*She puts her finger on her wrist.*] It's perfectly regular.

C.-C. When I suggested staying to luncheon Arnold looked exactly like a dose of castor oil.

Elizabeth. I wish you'd sit down.

C.-C. Will it make it easier for you? [*He takes a chair.*] You have evidently something very disagreeable to say to me.

Elizabeth. You won't be cross with me?

C.-C. How old are you?

Elizabeth. Twenty-five.

C.-C. I'm never cross with a woman under thirty.

Elizabeth. Oh, then I've got ten years.

C.-C. Mathematics?

Elizabeth. No. Paint.

C.-C. Well?

Elizabeth. [*Reflectively.*] I think it would be easier if I sat on your knees.

C.-C. That is a pleasing taste of yours, but you must take care not to put on weight.

[She sits down on his knees.]

Elizabeth. Am I boney?

C.-C. On the contrary. . . . I'm listening.

Elizabeth. Lady Catherine's coming here.

C.-C. Who's Lady Catherine?

Elizabeth. Your—Arnold's mother.

C.-C. Is she?

[He withdraws himself a little and Elizabeth gets up.]

Elizabeth. You mustn't blame Arnold. It's my fault. I insisted. He was against it. I nagged him till he gave way. And then I wrote and asked her to come.

C.-C. I didn't know you knew her.

Elizabeth. I don't. But I heard she was in London. She's staying at Claridge's. It seemed so heartless not to take the smallest notice of her.

C.-C. When is she coming?

Elizabeth. We're expecting her in time for luncheon.

C.-C. As soon as that? I understand the embarrassment.

Elizabeth. You see, we never expected you to be here. You said you'd be in Paris for another month.

C.-C. My dear child, this is your house. There's no reason why you shouldn't ask whom you please to stay with you.

Elizabeth. After all, whatever her faults, she's Arnold's

mother. It seemed so unnatural that they should never see one another. My heart ached for that poor lonely woman.

C.-C. I never heard that she was lonely, and she certainly isn't poor.

Elizabeth. And there's something else. I couldn't ask her by herself. It would have been so—so insulting. I asked Lord Porteous, too.

C.-C. I see.

Elizabeth. I daresay you'd rather not meet them.

C.-C. I daresay they'd rather not meet me. I shall get a capital luncheon at the cottage. I've noticed you always get the best food if you come in unexpectedly and have the same as they're having in the servants' hall.

Elizabeth. No one's ever talked to me about Lady Kitty. It's always been a subject that everyone has avoided. I've never even seen a photograph of her.

C.-C. The house was full of them when she left. I think I told the butler to throw them in the dust-bin. She was very much photographed.

Elizabeth. Won't you tell me what she was like?

C.-C. She was very like you, Elizabeth, only she had dark hair instead of red.

Elizabeth. Poor dear! it must be quite white now.

C.-C. I daresay. She was a pretty little thing.

Elizabeth. But she was one of the great beauties of her day. They say she was lovely.

C.-C. She had the most adorable little nose, like yours. . . .

Elizabeth. D'you like my nose?

C.-C. And she was very dainty, with a beautiful little figure; very light on her feet. She was like a *marquise* in an old French comedy. Yes, she was lovely.

Elizabeth. And I'm sure she's lovely still.

C.-C. She's no chicken, you know.

Elizabeth. You can't expect me to look at it as you and Arnold do. When you've loved as she's loved you may grow old, but you grow old beautifully.

C.-C. You're very romantic.

Elizabeth. If everyone hadn't made such a mystery of it I daresay I shouldn't feel as I do. I know she did a great wrong to you and a great wrong to Arnold. I'm willing to acknowledge that.

C.-C. I'm sure it's very kind of you.

Elizabeth. But she loved and she dared. Romance is such an illusive thing. You read of it in books, but it's seldom you see it face to face. I can't help it if it thrills me.

C.-C. I am painfully aware that the husband in these cases is not a romantic object.

Elizabeth. She had the world at her feet. You were rich. She was a figure in society. And she gave up everything for love.

C.-C. [*Dryly.*] I'm beginning to suspect it wasn't only for her sake and for Arnold's that you asked her to come here.

Elizabeth. I seem to know her already. I think her face is a little sad, for a love like that doesn't leave you gay, it leaves you grave, but I think her pale face is unlined. It's like a child's.

C.-C. My dear, how you let your imagination run away with you!

Elizabeth. I imagine her slight and frail.

C.-C. Frail, certainly.

Elizabeth. With beautiful thin hands and white hair. I've pictured her so often in that Renaissance Palace that they live in, with old Masters on the walls and lovely carved things all round, sitting in a black silk dress with old lace round her neck and old-fashioned diamonds. You see, I never knew my mother; she died when I was a baby. You can't confide in aunts with huge families of their own. I want Arnold's mother to be a mother to me. I've got so much to say to her.

C.-C. Are you happy with Arnold?

Elizabeth. Why shouldn't I be?

C.-C. Why haven't you got any babies?

Elizabeth. Give us a little time. We've only been married three years.

C.-C. I wonder what Hughie is like now!

Elizabeth. Lord Porteous?

C.-C. He wore his clothes better than any man in London. You know he'd have been Prime Minister if he'd remained in politics.

Elizabeth. What was he like then?

C.-C. He was a nice-looking fellow. Fine horseman. I suppose there was something very fascinating about him. Yellow hair and blue eyes, you know. He had a very good figure. I liked him. I was his parliamentary secretary. He was Arnold's godfather.

Elizabeth. I know.

C.-C. I wonder if he ever regrets!

Elizabeth. I wouldn't.

C.-C. Well, I must be strolling back to my cottage.

Elizabeth. You're not angry with me?

C.-C. Not a bit.

[*She puts up her face for him to kiss. He kisses her on both cheeks and then goes out. In a moment Teddie is seen at the window.*]

12

Teddie. I saw the old blighter go.

Elizabeth. Come in.

Teddie. Everything all right?

Elizabeth. Oh, quite, as far as he's concerned. He's going to keep out of the way.

Teddie. Was it beastly?

Elizabeth. No, he made it very easy for me. He's a nice old thing.

Teddie. You were rather scared.

Elizabeth. A little. I am still. I don't know why.

Teddie. I guessed you were. I thought I'd come and give you a little moral support. It's ripping here, isn't it?

Elizabeth. It is rather nice.

Teddie. It'll be jolly to think of it when I'm back in the F.M.S.

Elizabeth. Aren't you homesick sometimes?

Teddie. Oh, everyone is now and then, you know.

Elizabeth. You could have got a job in England if you'd wanted to, couldn't you?

Teddie. Oh, but I love it out there. England's ripping to come back to, but I couldn't live here now. It's like a woman you're desperately in love with as long as you don't see her, but when you're with her she maddens you so that you can't bear her.

Elizabeth. [*Smiling.*] What's wrong with England?

Teddie. I don't think anything's wrong with England. I expect something's wrong with me. I've been away too long. England seems to me full of people doing things they don't want to because other people expect it of them.

Elizabeth. Isn't that what you call a high degree of civilisation?

Teddie. People seem to me so insincere. When you go to parties in London they're all babbling about art, and you feel that in their hearts they don't care twopence about it. They read the books that everybody is talking about because they don't want to be out of it. In the F.M.S. we don't get very many books, and we read those we have over and over again. They mean so much to us. I don't think the people over there are half so clever as the people at home, but one gets to know them better. You see, there are so few of us that we have to make the best of one another.

Elizabeth. I imagine that frills are not much worn in the F.M.S. It must be a comfort.

Teddie. It's not much good being pretentious where everyone knows exactly who you are and what your income is.

Elizabeth. I don't think you want too much sincerity in society. It would be like an iron girder in a house of cards.

13

Teddie. And then, you know, the place is ripping. You get used to a blue sky and you miss it in England.

Elizabeth. What do you do with yourself all the time?

Teddie. Oh, one works like blazes. You have to be a pretty hefty fellow to be a planter. And then there's ripping bathing. You know, it's lovely, with palm trees all along the beach. And there's shooting. And now and then we have a little dance to a gramophone.

Elizabeth. [*Pretending to tease him.*] I think you've got a young woman out there, Teddie.

Teddie. [*Vehemently.*] Oh, no!

[*She is a little taken aback by the earnestness of his disclaimer. There is a moment's silence, then she recovers herself.*]

Elizabeth. But you'll have to marry and settle down one of these days, you know.

Teddie. I want to, but it's not a thing you can do lightly.

Elizabeth. I don't know why there more than elsewhere.

Teddie. In England if people don't get on they go their own ways and jog along after a fashion. In a place like that you're thrown a great deal on your own resources.

Elizabeth. Of course.

Teddie. Lots of girls come out because they think they're going to have a good time. But if they're empty-headed, then they're just faced with their own emptiness and they're done. If their husbands can afford it they go home and settle down as grass-widows.

Elizabeth. I've met them. They seem to find it a very pleasant occupation.

Teddie. It's rotten for their husbands, though.

Elizabeth. And if the husbands can't afford it?

Teddie. Oh, then they tipple.

Elizabeth. It's not a very alluring prospect.

Teddie. But if the woman's the right sort she wouldn't exchange it for any life in the world. When all's said and done it's we who've made the Empire.

Elizabeth. What sort is the right sort?

Teddie. A woman of courage and endurance and sincerity. Of course, it's hopeless unless she's in love with her husband.

[*He is looking at her earnestly and she, raising her eyes, gives him a long look. There is silence between them.*]

Teddie. My house stands on the side of a hill, and the cocoanut trees wind down to the shore. Azaleas grow in my garden,

14

and camellias, and all sorts of ripping flowers. And in front of me is the winding coast line, and then the blue sea.

[*A pause.*]

Do you know that I'm awfully in love with you?
Elizabeth. [*Gravely.*] I wasn't quite sure. I wondered.
Teddie. And you?

[*She nods slowly.*]

I've never kissed you.
Elizabeth. I don't want you to.

[*They look at one another steadily. They are both grave. Arnold comes in hurriedly.*]

Arnold. They're coming, Elizabeth.
Elizabeth. [*As though returning from a distant world.*] Who?
Arnold. [*Impatiently.*] My dear! My mother, of course. The car is just coming up the drive.
Teddie. Would you like me to clear out?
Arnold. No, no! For goodness' sake stay.
Elizabeth. We'd better go and meet them, Arnold.
Arnold. No, no; I think they'd much better be shown in. I feel simply sick with nervousness.

[*Anna comes in from the garden.*]

Anna. Your guests have arrived.
Elizabeth. Yes, I know.
Arnold. I've given orders that luncheon should be served at once.
Elizabeth. Why? It's not half-past one already, is it?
Arnold. I thought it would help. When you don't know exactly what to say you can always eat.

[*The Butler comes in and announces.*]

Butler. Lady Catherine Champion-Cheney! Lord Porteous!

[*Lady Kitty comes in followed by Porteous, and the Butler goes out. Lady Kitty is a gay little lady, with dyed red hair and painted cheeks. She is somewhat outrageously dressed. She never forgets*

15

that she has been a pretty woman and she still behaves as if she were twenty-five. Lord Porteous is a very bald, elderly gentleman in loose, rather eccentric clothes. He is snappy and gruff. This is not at all the couple that Elizabeth expected, and for a moment she stares at them with round, startled eyes. Lady Kitty goes up to her with outstretched hands.]

Lady Kitty. Elizabeth! Elizabeth! [*She kisses her effusively.*] What an adorable creature! [*Turning to Porteous.*] Hughie, isn't she adorable?

Porteous. [*With a grunt.*] Ugh!

[*Elizabeth, smiling now, turns to him and gives him her hand.*]

Elizabeth. How d'you do?

Porteous. Damnable road you've got down here. How d'you do, my dear? Why d'you have such damnable roads in England?

[*Lady Kitty's eyes fall on Teddie and she goes up to him with her arms thrown back, prepared to throw them round him.*]

Lady Kitty. My boy, my boy! I should have known you anywhere!

Elizabeth. [*Hastily.*] That's Arnold.

Lady Kitty. [*Without a moment's hesitation.*] The image of his father! I should have known him anywhere! [*She throws her arms round his neck.*] My boy, my boy!

Porteous. [*With a grunt.*] Ugh!

Lady Kitty. Tell me, would you have known me again? Have I changed?

Arnold. I was only five, you know, when—when you . . .

Lady Kitty. [*Emotionally.*] I remember as if it was yesterday. I went up into your room. [*With a sudden change of manner.*] By the way, I always thought that nurse drank. Did you ever find out if she really did?

Porteous. How the devil can you expect him to know that, Kitty?

Lady Kitty. You've never had a child, Hughie; how can you tell what they know and what they don't?

Elizabeth. [*Coming to the rescue.*] This is Arnold, Lord Porteous.

Porteous. [*Shaking hands with him.*] How d'you do? I knew your father.

Arnold. Yes.

16

Porteous. Alive still?

Arnold. Yes.

Porteous. He must be getting on. Is he well?

Arnold. Very.

Porteous. Ugh! Takes care of himself, I suppose. I'm not at all well. This damned climate doesn't agree with me.

Elizabeth. [*To Lady Kitty.*] This is Mrs. Shenstone. And this is Mr. Luton. I hope you don't mind a very small party.

Lady Kitty. [*Shaking hands with Anna and Teddie.*] Oh, no, I shall enjoy it. I used to give enormous parties here. Political, you know. How nice you've made this room!

Elizabeth. Oh, that's Arnold.

Arnold. [*Nervously.*] D'you like this chair? I've just bought it. It's exactly my period.

Porteous. [*Bluntly.*] It's a fake.

Arnold. [*Indignantly.*] I don't think it is for a minute.

Porteous. The legs are not right.

Arnold. I don't know how you can say that. If there is anything right about it, it's the legs.

Lady Kitty. I'm sure they're right.

Porteous. You know nothing whatever about it, Kitty.

Lady Kitty. That's what you think. *I* think it's a beautiful chair. Hepplewhite?

Arnold. No, Sheraton.

Lady Kitty. Oh, I know. "The School for Scandal."

Porteous. Sheraton, my dear. Sheraton.

Lady Kitty. Yes, that's what I say. I acted the screen scene at some amateur theatricals in Florence, and Ermeto Novelli, the great Italian tragedian, told me he'd never seen a Lady Teazle like me.

Porteous. Ugh!

Lady Kitty. [*To Elizabeth.*] Do you act?

Elizabeth. Oh, I couldn't. I should be too nervous.

Lady Kitty. I'm never nervous. I'm a born actress. Of course, if I had my time over again I'd go on the stage. You know, it's extraordinary how they keep young. Actresses, I mean. I think it's because they're always playing different parts. Hughie, do you think Arnold takes after me or after his father? Of course I think he's the very image of me. Arnold, I think I ought to tell you that I was received into the Catholic Church last winter. I'd been thinking about it for years, and last time we were at Monte Carlo I met such a nice monsignore. I told him what my difficulties were and he was too wonderful. I knew Hughie wouldn't approve, so I kept it a secret. [*To Elizabeth.*] Are you interested in religion? I think it's too

17

wonderful. We must have a long talk about it one of these days. [*Pointing to her frock.*] Callot?

Elizabeth. No, Worth.

Lady Kitty. I knew it was either Worth or Callot. Of course, it's line that's the important thing. I go to Worth myself, and I always say to him, "Line, my dear Worth, line." What *is* the matter, Hughie?

Porteous. These new teeth of mine are so damned uncomfortable.

Lady Kitty. Men are extraordinary. They can't stand the smallest discomfort. Why, a woman's life is uncomfortable from the moment she gets up in the morning till the moment she goes to bed at night. And d'you think it's comfortable to sleep with a mask on your face?

Porteous. They don't seem to hold up properly.

Lady Kitty. Well, that's not the fault of your teeth. That's the fault of your gums.

Porteous. Damned rotten dentist. That's what's the matter.

Lady Kitty. I thought he was a very nice dentist. He told me *my* teeth would last till I was fifty. He has a Chinese room. It's so interesting; while he scrapes your teeth he tells you all about the dear Empress Dowager. Are you interested in China? I think it's too wonderful. You know they've cut off their pigtails. I think it's such a pity. They were so picturesque.

[The Butler comes in.]

Butler. Luncheon is served, sir.

Elizabeth. Would you like to see your rooms?

Porteous. We can see our rooms after luncheon.

Lady Kitty. I must powder my nose, Hughie.

Porteous. Powder it down here.

Lady Kitty. I never saw anyone so inconsiderate.

Porteous. You'll keep us all waiting half an hour. I know you.

Lady Kitty. [*Fumbling in her bag.*] Oh, well, peace at any price, as Lord Beaconsfield said.

Porteous. He said a lot of damned silly things, Kitty, but he never said that.

[Lady Kitty's face changes. Perplexity is followed by dismay, and dismay by consternation.]

Lady Kitty. Oh!

Elizabeth. What is the matter?

18

Lady Kitty. [*With anguish.*] My lip-stick!

Elizabeth. Can't you find it?

Lady Kitty. I had it in the car. Hughie, you remember that I had it in the car.

Porteous. I don't remember anything about it.

Lady Kitty. Don't be so stupid, Hughie. Why, when we came through the gates I said: "My home, my home!" and I took it out and put some on my lips.

Elizabeth. Perhaps you dropped it in the car.

Lady Kitty. For heaven's sake send some one to look for it.

Arnold. I'll ring.

Lady Kitty. I'm absolutely lost without my lip-stick. Lend me yours, darling, will you?

Elizabeth. I'm awfully sorry. I'm afraid I haven't got one.

Lady Kitty. Do you mean to say you don't use a lip-stick?

Elizabeth. Never.

Porteous. Look at her lips. What the devil d'you think she wants muck like that for?

Lady Kitty. Oh, my dear, what a mistake you make! You *must* use a lip-stick. It's so good for the lips. Men like it, you know. I couldn't *live* without a lip-stick.

[*Champion-Cheney appears at the window holding in his upstretched hand a little gold case.*]

C.-C. [*As he comes in.*] Has anyone here lost a diminutive utensil containing, unless I am mistaken, a favourite preparation for the toilet?

[*Arnold and Elizabeth are thunderstruck at his appearance and even Teddie and Anna are taken aback. But Lady Kitty is overjoyed.*]

Lady Kitty. My lip-stick!

C.-C. I found it in the drive and I ventured to bring it in.

Lady Kitty. It's Saint Antony. I said a little prayer to him when I was hunting in my bag.

Porteous. Saint Antony be blowed! It's Clive, by God!

Lady Kitty. [*Startled, her attention suddenly turning from the lip-stick.*] Clive!

C.-C. You didn't recognise me. It's many years since we met.

Lady Kitty. My poor Clive, your hair has gone quite white!

C.-C. [*Holding out his hand.*] I hope you had a pleasant journey down from London.

19

Lady Kitty. [*Offering him her cheek.*] You may kiss me, Clive.

C.-C. [*Kissing her.*] You don't mind, Hughie?

Porteous. [*With a grunt.*] Ugh!

C.-C. [*Going up to him cordially.*] And how are you, my dear Hughie?

Porteous. Damned rheumatic if you want to know. Filthy climate you have in this country.

C.-C. Aren't you going to shake hands with me, Hughie?

Porteous. I have no objection to shaking hands with you.

C.-C. You've aged, my poor Hughie.

Porteous. Some one was asking me how old you were the other day.

C.-C. Were they surprised when you told them?

Porteous. Surprised! They wondered you weren't dead.

[*The Butler comes in.*]

Butler. Did you ring, sir?

Arnold. No. Oh, yes, I did. It doesn't matter now.

C.-C. [*As the Butler is going.*] One moment. My dear Elizabeth, I've come to throw myself on your mercy. My servants are busy with their own affairs. There's not a thing for me to eat in my cottage.

Elizabeth. Oh, but we shall be delighted if you'll lunch with us.

C.-C. It either means that or my immediate death from starvation. You don't mind, Arnold?

Arnold. My dear father!

Elizabeth. [*To the Butler.*] Mr. Cheney will lunch here.

Butler. Very good, ma'am.

C.-C. [*To Lady Kitty.*] And what do you think of Arnold?

Lady Kitty. I adore him.

C.-C. He's grown, hasn't he? But then you'd expect him to do that in thirty years.

Arnold. For God's sake let's go in to lunch, Elizabeth!

END OF THE FIRST ACT

THE SECOND ACT

The Scene is the same as in the preceding Act.

It is afternoon. When the curtain rises Porteous and Lady Kitty, Anna and Teddie are playing bridge. Elizabeth and Champion-Cheney are watching. Porteous and Lady Kitty are partners.

C.-C. When will Arnold be back, Elizabeth?

Elizabeth. Soon, I think.

C.-C. Is he addressing a meeting?

Elizabeth. No, it's only a conference with his agent and one or two constituents.

Porteous. [*Irritably.*] How anyone can be expected to play bridge when people are shouting at the top of their voices all round them, I for one cannot understand.

Elizabeth. [*Smiling.*] I'm so sorry.

Anna. I can see your hand, Lord Porteous.

Porteous. It may help you.

Lady Kitty. I've told you over and over again to hold your cards up. It ruins one's game when one can't help seeing one's opponent's hand.

Porteous. One isn't obliged to look.

Lady Kitty. What was Arnold's majority at the last election?

Elizabeth. Seven hundred and something.

C.-C. He'll have to fight for it if he wants to keep his seat next time.

Porteous. Are we playing bridge, or talking politics?

Lady Kitty. I never find that conversation interferes with my game.

Porteous. You certainly play no worse when you talk than when you hold your tongue.

Lady Kitty. I think that's a very offensive thing to say, Hughie. Just because I don't play the same game as you do you think I can't play.

Porteous. I'm glad you acknowledge it's not the same game as I play. But why in God's name do you call it bridge?

C.-C. I agree with Kitty. I hate people who play bridge as though they were at a funeral and knew their feet were getting wet.

Porteous. Of course you take Kitty's part.

Lady Kitty. That's the least he can do.

21

C.-C. I have a naturally cheerful disposition.

Porteous. You've never had anything to sour it.

Lady Kitty. I don't know what you mean by that, Hughie.

Porteous. [*Trying to contain himself.*] Must you trump my ace?

Lady Kitty. [*Innocently.*] Oh, was that your ace, darling?

Porteous. [*Furiously.*] Yes, it was my ace.

Lady Kitty. Oh, well, it was the only trump I had. I shouldn't have made it anyway.

Porteous. You needn't have told them that. Now she knows exactly what I've got.

Lady Kitty. She knew before.

Porteous. How could she know?

Lady Kitty. She said she'd seen your hand.

Anna. Oh, I didn't. I said I could see it.

Lady Kitty. Well, I naturally supposed that if she could see it she did.

Porteous. Really, Kitty, you have the most extraordinary ideas.

C.-C. Not at all. If anyone is such a fool as to show me his hand, of course I look at it.

Porteous. [*Fuming.*] If you study the etiquette of bridge, you'll discover that onlookers are expected not to interfere with the game.

C.-C. My dear Hughie, this is a matter of ethics, not of bridge.

Anna. Anyhow, I get the game. And rubber.

Teddie. I claim a revoke.

Porteous. Who revoked?

Teddie. You did.

Porteous. Nonsense. I've never revoked in my life.

Teddie. I'll show you. [*He turns over the tricks to show the faces of the cards.*] You threw away a club on the third heart trick and you had another heart.

Porteous. I never had more than two hearts.

Teddie. Oh, yes, you had. Look here. That's the card you played on the last trick but one.

Lady Kitty. [*Delighted to catch him out.*] There's no doubt about it, Hughie. You revoked.

Porteous. I tell you I did not revoke. I never revoke.

C.-C. You did, Hughie. I wondered what on earth you were doing.

Porteous. I don't know how anyone can be expected not to revoke when there's this confounded chatter going on all the time.

Teddie. Well, that's another hundred to us.

Porteous. [*To Champion-Cheney.*] I wish you wouldn't

22

breathe down my neck. I never can play bridge when there's somebody breathing down my neck.

[*The party have risen from the bridge-table, and they scatter about the room.*]

Anna. Well, I'm going to take a book and lie down in the hammock till it's time to dress.

Teddie. [*Who has been adding up.*] I'll put it down in the book, shall I?

Porteous. [*Who has not moved, setting out the cards for a patience.*] Yes, yes, put it down. I never revoke.

[*Anna goes out.*

Lady Kitty. Would you like to come for a little stroll, Hughie?

Porteous. What for?

Lady Kitty. Exercise.

Porteous. I hate exercise.

C.-C. [*Looking at the patience.*] The seven goes on the eight.

[*Porteous takes no notice.*]

Lady Kitty. The seven goes on the eight, Hughie.

Porteous. I don't choose to put the seven on the eight.

C.-C. That knave goes on the queen.

Porteous. I'm not blind, thank you.

Lady Kitty. The three goes on the four.

C.-C. All these go over.

Porteous. [*Furiously.*] Am I playing this patience, or are you playing it?

Lady Kitty. But you're missing everything.

Porteous. That's my business.

C.-C. It's no good losing your temper over it, Hughie.

Porteous. Go away, both of you. You irritate me.

Lady Kitty. We were only trying to help you, Hughie.

Porteous. I don't want to be helped. I want to do it by myself.

Lady Kitty. I think your manners are perfectly deplorable, Hughie.

Porteous. It's simply maddening when you're playing patience and people won't leave you alone.

C.-C. We won't say another word.

Porteous. That three goes. I believe it's coming out. If I'd been such a fool as to put that seven up I shouldn't have been able to bring these down.

23

[He puts down several cards while they watch him silently.]

Lady Kitty and C.-C. [*Together.*] The four goes on the five.

Porteous. [*Throwing down the cards violently.*] Damn you! why don't you leave me alone? It's intolerable.

C.-C. It was coming out, my dear fellow.

Porteous. I know it was coming out. Confound you!

Lady Kitty. How petty you are, Hughie!

Porteous. Petty, be damned! I've told you over and over again that I will not be interfered with when I'm playing patience.

Lady Kitty. Don't talk to me like that, Hughie.

Porteous. I shall talk to you as I please.

Lady Kitty. [*Beginning to cry.*] Oh, you brute! You brute! [*She flings out of the room.*]

Porteous. Oh, damn! now she's going to cry.

[He shambles out into the garden. Champion-Cheney, Elizabeth and Teddie are left alone. There is a moment's pause. Champion-Cheney looks from Teddie to Elizabeth, with an ironical smile.]

C.-C. Upon my soul, they might be married. They frip so much.

Elizabeth. [*Frigidly.*] It's been nice of you to come here so often since they arrived. It's helped to make things easy.

C.-C. Irony? It's a rhetorical form not much favoured in this blessed plot, this earth, this realm, this England.

Elizabeth. What exactly are you getting at?

C.-C. How slangy the young women of the present day are! I suppose the fact that Arnold is a purist leads you to the contrary extravagance.

Elizabeth. Anyhow you know what I mean.

C.-C. [*With a smile.*] I have a dim, groping suspicion.

Elizabeth. You promised to keep away. Why did you come back the moment they arrived?

C.-C. Curiosity, my dear child. A surely pardonable curiosity.

Elizabeth. And since then you've been here all the time. You don't generally favour us with so much of your company when you're down at your cottage.

C.-C. I've been excessively amused.

Elizabeth. It has struck me that whenever they started fripping you took a malicious pleasure in goading them on.

C.-C. I don't think there's much love lost between them now, do you?

24

[Teddie is making as though to leave the room.]

Elizabeth. Don't go, Teddie.

C.-C. No, please don't. I'm only staying a minute. We were talking about Lady Kitty just before she arrived. [*To Elizabeth.*] Do you remember? The pale, frail lady in black satin and old lace.

Elizabeth. [*With a chuckle.*] You are a devil, you know.

C.-C. Ah, well, he's always had the reputation of being a humorist and a gentleman.

Elizabeth. Did *you* expect her to be like that, poor dear?

C.-C. My dear child, I hadn't the vaguest idea. You were asking me the other day what she was like when she ran away. I didn't tell you half. She was so gay and so natural. Who would have thought that animation would turn into such frivolity, and that charming impulsiveness lead to such a ridiculous affectation?

Elizabeth. It rather sets my nerves on edge to hear the way you talk of her.

C.-C. It's the truth that sets your nerves on edge, not I.

Elizabeth. You loved her once. Have you no feeling for her at all?

C.-C. None. Why should I?

Elizabeth. She's the mother of your son.

C.-C. My dear child, you have a charming nature, as simple, frank, and artless as hers was. Don't let pure humbug obscure your common sense.

Elizabeth. We have no right to judge. She's only been here two days. We know nothing about her.

C.-C. My dear, her soul is as thickly rouged as her face. She hasn't an emotion that's sincere. She's tinsel. You think I'm a cruel, cynical old man. Why, when I think of what she was, if I didn't laugh at what she has become I should cry.

Elizabeth. How do you know she wouldn't be just the same now if she'd remained your wife? Do you think your influence would have had such a salutary effect on her?

C.-C. [*Good-humouredly.*] I like you when you're bitter and rather insolent.

Elizabeth. D'you like me enough to answer my question?

C.-C. She was only twenty-seven when she went away. She might have become anything. She might have become the woman you expected her to be. There are very few of us who are strong enough to make circumstances serve us. We are the creatures of our environment. She's a silly, worthless woman because she's led a silly, worthless life.

Elizabeth. [*Disturbed.*] You're horrible to-day.

C.-C. I don't say it's I who could have prevented her from becoming this ridiculous caricature of a pretty woman grown old. But life could. Here she would have had the friends fit to her station, and a decent activity, and worthy interests. Ask her what her life has been all these years among divorced women and kept women and the men who consort with them. There is no more lamentable pursuit than a life of pleasure.

Elizabeth. At all events she loved and she loved greatly. I have only pity and affection for her.

C.-C. And if she loved what d'you think she felt when she saw that she had ruined Hughie? Look at him. He was tight last night after dinner and tight the night before.

Elizabeth. I know.

C.-C. And she took it as a matter of course. How long do you suppose he's been getting tight every night? Do you think he was like that thirty years ago? Can you imagine that that was a brilliant young man, whom everyone expected to be Prime Minister? Look at him now. A grumpy sodden old fellow with false teeth.

Elizabeth. You have false teeth, too.

C.-C. Yes, but damn it all, they fit. She's ruined him and she knows she's ruined him.

Elizabeth. [*Looking at him suspiciously.*] Why are you saying all this to me?

C.-C. Am I hurting your feelings?

Elizabeth. I think I've had enough for the present.

C.-C. I'll go and have a look at the gold-fish. I want to see Arnold when he comes in. [*Politely.*] I'm afraid we've been boring Mr. Luton.

Teddie. Not at all.

C.-C. When are you going back to the F.M.S.?

Teddie. In about a month.

C.-C. I see.

[*He goes out.*]

Elizabeth. I wonder what he has at the back of his head.

Teddie. D'you think he was talking at you?

Elizabeth. He's as clever as a bagful of monkeys.

[*There is a moment's pause. Teddie hesitates a little and when he speaks it is in a different tone. He is grave and somewhat nervous.*]

Teddie. It seems very difficult to get a few minutes alone with you. I wonder if you've been making it difficult?

26

Elizabeth. I wanted to think.

Teddie. I've made up my mind to go away to-morrow.

Elizabeth. Why?

Teddie. I want you altogether or not at all.

Elizabeth. You're so arbitrary.

Teddie. You said you—you said you cared for me.

Elizabeth. I do.

Teddie. Do you mind if we talk it over now?

Elizabeth. No.

Teddie. [*Frowning.*] It makes me feel rather shy and awkward. I've repeated to myself over and over again exactly what I want to say to you, and now all I'd prepared seems rather footling.

Elizabeth. I'm so afraid I'm going to cry.

Teddie. I feel it's all so tremendously serious and I think we ought to keep emotion out of it. You're rather emotional, aren't you?

Elizabeth. [*Half smiling and half in tears.*] So are you for the matter of that.

Teddie. That's why I wanted to have everything I meant to say to you cut and dried. I think it would be awfully unfair if I made love to you and all that sort of thing, and you were carried away. I wrote it all down and thought I'd send it you as a letter.

Elizabeth. Why didn't you?

Teddie. I got the wind up. A letter seems so—so cold. You see, I love you so awfully.

Elizabeth. For goodness' sake don't say that.

Teddie. You mustn't cry. Please don't, or I shall go all to pieces.

Elizabeth. [*Trying to smile.*] I'm sorry. It doesn't mean anything really. It's only tears running out of my eyes.

Teddie. Our only chance is to be awfully matter-of-fact.

[*He stops for a moment. He finds it quite difficult to control himself. He clears his throat. He frowns with annoyance at himself.*]

Elizabeth. What's the matter?

Teddie. I've got a sort of lump in my throat. It is idiotic. I think I'll have a cigarette.

[*She watches him in silence while he lights a cigarette.*]

You see, I've never been in love with anyone before, not really. It's knocked me endways. I don't know how I can live without you now. . . . Does that old fool know I'm in love with you?

27

Elizabeth. I think so.

Teddie. When he was talking about Lady Kitty smashing up Lord Porteous' career I thought there was something at the back of it.

Elizabeth. I think he was trying to persuade me not to smash up yours.

Teddie. I'm sure that's very considerate of him, but I don't happen to have one to smash. I wish I had. It's the only time in my life I've wished I were a hell of a swell so that I could chuck it all and show you how much more you are to me than anything else in the world.

Elizabeth. [*Affectionately.*] You're a dear old thing, Teddie.

Teddie. You know, I don't really know how to make love, but if I did I couldn't do it now because I just want to be absolutely practical.

Elizabeth. [*Chaffing him.*] I'm glad you don't know how to make love. It would be almost more than I could bear.

Teddie. You see, I'm not at all romantic and that sort of thing. I'm just a common or garden business man. All this is so dreadfully serious and I think we ought to be sensible.

Elizabeth. [*With a break in her voice.*] You owl!

Teddie. No, Elizabeth, don't say things like that to me. I want you to consider all the *pros* and *cons,* and my heart's thumping against my chest, and you know I love you, I love you, I love you.

Elizabeth. [*In a sigh of passion.*] Oh, my precious!

Teddie. [*Impatiently, but with himself, rather than with Elizabeth.*] Don't be idiotic, Elizabeth. I'm not going to tell you that I can't live without you and a lot of muck like that. You know that you mean everything in the world to me. [*Almost giving it up as a bad job.*] Oh, my God!

Elizabeth. [*Her voice faltering.*] D'you think there's anything you can say to me that I don't know already?

Teddie. [*Desperately.*] But I haven't said a single thing I wanted to. I'm a business man and I want to put it all in a business way, if you understand what I mean.

Elizabeth. [*Smiling.*] I don't believe you're a very good business man.

Teddie. [*Sharply.*] You don't know what you're talking about. I'm a first-rate business man, but somehow this is different. [*Hopelessly.*] I don't know why it won't go right.

Elizabeth. What are we going to do about it?

Teddie. You see, it's not just because you're awfully pretty that I love you. I'd love you just as much if you were old and ugly. It's you I love, not what you look like. And it's not only love; love be blowed! It's that I *like* you so tremendously. I think you're such a ripping good sort. I just want to be with you. I feel so jolly and happy just to think you're there. I'm so awfully *fond* of you.

Elizabeth. [*Laughing through her tears.*] I don't know if this is your idea of introducing a business proposition.

Teddie. Damn you, you won't let me.

Elizabeth. You said "Damn you."

Teddie. I meant it.

Elizabeth. Your voice sounded as if you meant it, you perfect duck!

Teddie. Really, Elizabeth, you're intolerable.

Elizabeth. I'm doing nothing.

Teddie. Yes, you are, you're putting me off my blow. What I want to say is perfectly simple. I'm a very ordinary business man.

Elizabeth. You've said that before.

Teddie. [*Angrily.*] Shut up. I haven't got a bob besides what I earn. I've got no position. I'm nothing. You're rich and you're a big pot and you've got everything that anyone can want. It's awful cheek my saying anything to you at all. But after all there's only one thing that really matters in the world, and that's love. I love you. Chuck all this, Elizabeth, and come to me.

Elizabeth. Are you cross with me?

Teddie. Furious.

Elizabeth. Darling!

Teddie. If you don't want me tell me so at once and let me get out quickly.

Elizabeth. Teddie, nothing in the world matters anything to me but you. I'll go wherever you take me. I love you.

Teddie. [*All to pieces.*] Oh, my God!

Elizabeth. Does it mean as much to you as that? Oh, Teddie!

Teddie. [*Trying to control himself.*] Don't be a fool, Elizabeth.

Elizabeth. It's you're the fool. You're making me cry.

Teddie. You're so damned emotional.

Elizabeth. Damned emotional yourself. I'm sure you're a rotten business man.

Teddie. I don't care what you think. You've made me so awfully happy. I say, what a lark life's going to be!

Elizabeth. Teddie, you are an angel.

Teddie. Let's get out quick. It's no good wasting time. Elizabeth.

Elizabeth. What?

Teddie. Nothing. I just like to say Elizabeth.

Elizabeth. You fool!

Teddie. I say, can you shoot?

Elizabeth. No.

Teddie. I'll teach you. You don't know how ripping it is to start out from your camp at dawn and travel through the jungle. And you're so tired at night and the sky's all starry. It's a fair treat. Of course I didn't want to say anything about all that till you'd decided. I'd made up my mind to be absolutely practical.

Elizabeth. [*Chaffing him.*] The only practical thing you said was that love is the only thing that really matters.

Teddie. [*Happily.*] Pull the other leg next time, will you? I should have to have one longer than the other.

Elizabeth. Isn't it fun being in love with some one who's in love with you?

Teddie. I say, I think I'd better clear out at once, don't you? It seems rather rotten to stay on in—in this house.

Elizabeth. You can't go to-night. There's no train.

Teddie. I'll go to-morrow. I'll wait in London till you're ready to join me.

Elizabeth. I'm not going to leave a note on the pincushion like Lady Kitty, you know. I'm going to tell Arnold.

Teddie. Are you? Don't you think there'll be an awful bother?

Elizabeth. I must face it. I should hate to be sly and deceitful.

Teddie. Well, then, let's face it together.

Elizabeth. No, I'll talk to Arnold by myself.

Teddie. You won't let anyone influence you?

Elizabeth. No.

[*He holds out his hand and she takes it. They look into one another's eyes with grave, almost solemn affection. There is the sound outside of a car driving up.*]

Elizabeth. There's the car. Arnold's come back. I must go and bathe my eyes. I don't want them to see I've been crying.

Teddie. All right. [*As she is going.*] Elizabeth.

Elizabeth. [*Stopping.*] What?

Teddie. Bless you.

Elizabeth. [*Affectionately.*] Idiot!

[*She goes out of the door and Teddie through the French window into the garden. For an instant the room is empty. Arnold comes in. He sits down and takes some papers out of his despatch-case. Lady Kitty enters. He gets up.*]

Lady Kitty. I saw you come in. Oh, my dear, don't get up. There's no reason why you should be so dreadfully polite to me.

Arnold. I've just rung for a cup of tea.

Lady Kitty. Perhaps we shall have the chance of a little talk. We don't seem to have had five minutes by ourselves. I want to make your acquaintance, you know.

Arnold. I should like you to know that it's not by my wish that my father is here.

Lady Kitty. But I'm so interested to see him.

Arnold. I was afraid that you and Lord Porteous must find it embarrassing.

Lady Kitty. Oh, no. Hughie was his greatest friend. They were at Eton and Oxford together. I think your father has improved so much since I saw him last. He wasn't good-looking as a young man, but now he's quite handsome.

[*The Footman brings in a tray on which are tea-things.*]

Lady Kitty. Shall I pour it out for you?

Arnold. Thank you very much.

Lady Kitty. Do you take sugar?

Arnold. No. I gave it up during the war.

Lady Kitty. So wise of you. It's so bad for the figure. Besides being patriotic, of course. Isn't it absurd that I should ask my son if he takes sugar or not? Life is really very quaint. Sad, of course, but oh, so quaint! Often I lie in bed at night and have a good laugh to myself as I think how quaint life is.

Arnold. I'm afraid I'm a very serious person.

Lady Kitty. How old are you now, Arnold?

Arnold. Thirty-five.

Lady Kitty. Are you really? Of course, I was a child when I married your father.

Arnold. Really. He always told me you were twenty-two.

Lady Kitty. Oh, what nonsense! Why, I was married out of the nursery. I put my hair up for the first time on my wedding-day.

Arnold. Where is Lord Porteous?

Lady Kitty. My dear, it sounds too absurd to hear you call him Lord Porteous. Why don't you call him—Uncle Hughie?

Arnold. He doesn't happen to be my uncle.

Lady Kitty. No, but he's your godfather. You know, I'm sure you'll like him when you know him better. I'm so hoping that you and Elizabeth will come and stay with us in Florence. I simply adore Elizabeth. She's too beautiful.

Arnold. Her hair is very pretty.

Lady Kitty. It's not touched up, is it?

Arnold. Oh, no.

31

Lady Kitty. I just wondered. It's rather a coincidence that her hair should be the same colour as mine. I suppose it shows that your father and you are attracted by just the same thing. So interesting, heredity, isn't it?

Arnold. Very.

Lady Kitty. Of course, since I joined the Catholic Church I don't believe in it any more. Darwin and all that sort of thing. Too dreadful. Wicked, you know. Besides, it's not very good form, is it?

[Champion-Cheney comes in from the garden.]

C.-C. Do I intrude?

Lady Kitty. Come in, Clive. Arnold and I have been having such a wonderful heart-to-heart talk.

C.-C. Very nice.

Arnold. Father, I stepped in for a moment at the Harveys' on my way back. It's simply criminal what they're doing with that house.

C.-C. What are they doing?

Arnold. It's an almost perfect Georgian house and they've got a lot of dreadful Victorian furniture. I gave them my ideas on the subject, but it's quite hopeless. They said they were attached to their furniture.

C.-C. Arnold should have been an interior decorator.

Lady Kitty. He has wonderful taste. He gets that from me.

Arnold. I suppose I have a certain *flair*. I have a passion for decorating houses.

Lady Kitty. You've made this one charming.

C.-C. D'you remember, we just had chintzes and comfortable chairs when we lived here, Kitty.

Lady Kitty. Perfectly hideous, wasn't it?

C.-C. In those days gentlemen and ladies were not expected to have taste.

Arnold. You know, I've been looking at this chair again. Since Lord Porteous said the legs weren't right I've been very uneasy.

Lady Kitty. He only said that because he was in a bad temper.

C.-C. His temper seems to me very short these days, Kitty.

Lady Kitty. Oh, it is.

Arnold. You feel he knows what he's talking about. I gave seventy-five pounds for that chair. I'm very seldom taken in. I always think if a thing's right you feel it.

C.-C. Well, don't let it disturb your night's rest.

Arnold. But, my dear father, that's just what it does. I had a most horrible dream about it last night.

32

Lady Kitty. Here is Hughie.

Arnold. I'm going to fetch a book I have on Old English furniture. There's an illustration of a chair which is almost identical with this one.

[Porteous comes in.]

Porteous. Quite a family gathering, by George!

C.-C. I was thinking just now we'd make a very pleasing picture of a typical English home.

Arnold. I'll be back in five minutes. There's something I want to show you, Lord Porteous.

[He goes out.]

C.-C. Would you like to play piquet with me, Hughie?

Porteous. Not particularly.

C.-C. You were never much of a piquet player, were you?

Porteous. My dear Clive, you people don't know what piquet is in England.

C.-C. Let's have a game then. You may make money.

Porteous. I don't want to play with you.

Lady Kitty. I don't know why not, Hughie.

Porteous. Let me tell you that I don't like your manner.

C.-C. I'm sorry for that. I'm afraid I can't offer to change it at my age.

Porteous. I don't know what you want to be hanging around here for.

C.-C. A natural attachment to my home.

Porteous. If you'd had any tact you'd have kept out of the way while we were here.

C.-C. My dear Hughie, I don't understand your attitude at all. If I'm willing to let bygones be bygones why should you object?

Porteous. Damn it all, they're not bygones.

C.-C. After all, I am the injured party.

Porteous. How the devil are you the injured party?

C.-C. Well, you did run away with my wife, didn't you?

Lady Kitty. Now, don't let's go into ancient history. I can't see why we shouldn't all be friends.

Porteous. I beg you not to interfere, Kitty.

Lady Kitty. I'm very fond of Clive.

Porteous. You never cared two straws for Clive. You only say that to irritate me.

Lady Kitty. Not at all. I don't see why he shouldn't come and stay with us.

C.-C. I'd love to. I think Florence in spring-time is delightful. Have you central heating?

Porteous. I never liked you, I don't like you now, and I never shall like you.

C.-C. How very unfortunate! because I liked you, I like you now, and I shall continue to like you.

Lady Kitty. There's something very nice about you, Clive.

Porteous. If you think that, why the devil did you leave him?

Lady Kitty. Are you going to reproach me because I loved you? How utterly, utterly, utterly detestable you are!

C.-C. Now, now, don't quarrel with one another.

Lady Kitty. It's all his fault. I'm the easiest person in the world to live with. But really he'd try the patience of a saint.

C.-C. Come, come, don't get upset, Kitty. When two people live together there must be a certain amount of give and take.

Porteous. I don't know what the devil you're talking about.

C.-C. It hasn't escaped my observation that you are a little inclined to frip. Many couples are. I think it's a pity.

Porteous. Would you have the very great kindness to mind your own business?

Lady Kitty. It is his business. He naturally wants me to be happy.

C.-C. I have the very greatest affection for Kitty.

Porteous. Then why the devil didn't you look after her properly?

C.-C. My dear Hughie, you were my greatest friend. I trusted you. It may have been rash.

Porteous. It was inexcusable.

Lady Kitty. I don't know what you mean by that, Hughie.

Porteous. Don't, don't, don't try and bully me, Kitty.

Lady Kitty. Oh, I know what you mean.

Porteous. Then why the devil did you say you didn't?

Lady Kitty. When I think that I sacrificed everything for that man! And for thirty years I've had to live in a filthy marble palace with no sanitary conveniences.

C.-C. D'you mean to say you haven't got a bathroom?

Lady Kitty. I've had to wash in a tub.

C.-C. My poor Kitty, how you've suffered!

Porteous. Really, Kitty, I'm sick of hearing of the sacrifices you made. I suppose you think I sacrificed nothing. I should have been Prime Minister by now if it hadn't been for you.

Lady Kitty. Nonsense!

Porteous. What do you mean by that? Everyone said I should be Prime Minister. Shouldn't I have been Prime Minister, Clive?

C.-C. It was certainly the general expectation.

Porteous. I was the most promising young man of my day. I was bound to get a seat in the Cabinet at the next election.

Lady Kitty. They'd have found you out just as I've found you out. I'm sick of hearing that I ruined your career. You never had a career to ruin. Prime Minister! You haven't the brain. You haven't the character.

C.-C. Cheek, push, and a gift of the gab will serve very well instead, you know.

Lady Kitty. Besides, in politics it's not the men that matter. It's the women at the back of them. I could have made Clive a Cabinet Minister if I'd wanted to.

Porteous. Clive?

Lady Kitty. With my beauty, my charm, my force of character, my wit, I could have done anything.

Porteous. Clive was nothing but my political secretary. When I was Prime Minister I might have made him Governor of some Colony or other. Western Australia, say. Out of pure kindliness.

Lady Kitty. [*With flashing eyes.*] D'you think I would have buried myself in Western Australia? With my beauty? My charm?

Porteous. Or Barbadoes, perhaps.

Lady Kitty. [*Furiously.*] Barbadoes! Barbadoes can go to—Barbadoes.

Porteous. That's all you'd have got.

Lady Kitty. Nonsense! I'd have India.

Porteous. I would never have given you India.

Lady Kitty. You would have given me India.

Porteous. I tell you I wouldn't.

Lady Kitty. The King would have given me India. The nation would have insisted on my having India. I would have been a vice-reine or nothing.

Porteous. I tell you that as long as the interests of the British Empire—Damn it all, my teeth are coming out!

[*He hurries from the room.*]

Lady Kitty. It's too much. I can't bear it any more. I've put up with him for thirty years and now I'm at the end of my tether.

C.-C. Calm yourself, my dear Kitty.

Lady Kitty. I won't listen to a word. I've quite made up my mind. It's finished, finished, finished. [*With a change of tone.*] I was so touched when I heard that you never lived in this house again after I left it.

C.-C. The cuckoos have always been very plentiful. Their note has a personal application which, I must say, I have found extremely offensive.

Lady Kitty. When I saw that you didn't marry again I couldn't help thinking that you still loved me.

C.-C. I am one of the few men I know who is able to profit by experience.

Lady Kitty. In the eyes of the Church I am still your wife. The Church is so wise. It knows that in the end a woman always comes back to her first love. Clive, I am willing to return to you.

C.-C. My dear Kitty, I couldn't take advantage of your momentary vexation with Hughie to let you take a step which I know you would bitterly regret.

Lady Kitty. You've waited for me a long time. For Arnold's sake.

C.-C. Do you think we really need bother about Arnold? In the last thirty years he's had time to grow used to the situation.

Lady Kitty. [*With a little smile.*] I think I've sown my wild oats, Clive.

C.-C. I haven't. I was a good young man, Kitty.

Lady Kitty. I know.

C.-C. And I'm very glad, because it has enabled me to be a wicked old one.

Lady Kitty. I beg your pardon.

[*Arnold comes in with a large book in his hand.*]

Arnold. I say, I've found the book I was hunting for. Oh! isn't Lord Porteous here?

Lady Kitty. One moment, Arnold. Your father and I are busy.

Arnold. I'm so sorry.

[*He goes out into the garden.*]

Lady Kitty. Explain yourself, Clive.

C.-C. When you ran away from me, Kitty, I was sore and angry and miserable. But above all I felt a fool.

Lady Kitty. Men are so vain.

C.-C. But I was a student of history, and presently I reflected that I shared my misfortune with very nearly all the greatest men.

Lady Kitty. I'm a great reader myself. It has always struck me as peculiar.

C.-C. The explanation is very simple. Women dislike intelligence, and when they find it in their husbands they revenge themselves on them in the only way they can, by making them— well, what you made me.

Lady Kitty. It's ingenious. It may be true.

C.-C. I felt I had done my duty by society and I determined to devote the rest of my life to my own entertainment. The House of Commons had always bored me excessively and the scandal of our divorce gave me an opportunity to resign my seat. I have been relieved to find that the country got on perfectly well without me.

Lady Kitty. But has love never entered your life?

C.-C. Tell me frankly, Kitty, don't you think people make a lot of unnecessary fuss about love?

Lady Kitty. It's the most wonderful thing in the world.

C.-C. You're incorrigible. Do you really think it was worth sacrificing so much for?

Lady Kitty. My dear Clive, I don't mind telling you that if I had my time over again I should be unfaithful to you, but I should not leave you.

C.-C. For some years I was notoriously the prey of a secret sorrow. But I found so many charming creatures who were anxious to console that in the end it grew rather fatiguing. Out of regard to my health I ceased to frequent the drawing-rooms of Mayfair.

Lady Kitty. And since then?

C.-C. Since then I have allowed myself the luxury of assisting financially a succession of dear little things, in a somewhat humble sphere, between the ages of twenty and twenty-five.

Lady Kitty. I cannot understand the infatuation of men for young girls. I think they're so dull.

C.-C. It's a matter of taste. I love old wine, old friends and old books, but I like young women. On their twenty-fifth birthday I give them a diamond ring and tell them they must no longer waste their youth and beauty on an old fogey like me. We have a most affecting scene, my technique on these occasions is perfect, and then I start all over again.

Lady Kitty. You're a wicked old man, Clive.

C.-C. That's what I told you. But, by George! I'm a happy one.

Lady Kitty. There's only one course open to me now.

C.-C. What is that?

Lady Kitty. [*With a flashing smile.*] To go and dress for dinner.

C.-C. Capital. I will follow your example.

[As Lady Kitty goes out Elizabeth comes in.]

Elizabeth. Where is Arnold?

C.-C. He's on the terrace. I'll call him.

Elizabeth. Don't bother.

C.-C. I was just strolling along to my cottage to put on a dinner jacket. [*As he goes out.*] Arnold.

[Exit C.-C.]

Arnold. Hulloa! [*He comes in.*] Oh, Elizabeth, I've found an illustration here of a chair which is almost identical with mine. It's dated 1750. Look!

Elizabeth. That's very interesting.

Arnold. I want to show it to Porteous. [*Moving a chair which has been misplaced.*] You know, it does exasperate me the way people will not leave things alone. I no sooner put a thing in its place than somebody moves it.

Elizabeth. It must be maddening for you.

Arnold. It is. You are the worst offender. I can't think why you don't take the pride that I do in the house. After all, it's one of the show places in the county.

Elizabeth. I'm afraid you find me very unsatisfactory.

Arnold. [*Good-humouredly.*] I don't know about that. But my two subjects are politics and decoration. I should be a perfect fool if I didn't see that you don't care two straws about either.

Elizabeth. We haven't very much in common, Arnold, have we?

Arnold. I don't think you can blame me for that.

Elizabeth. I don't. I blame you for nothing. I have no fault to find with you.

Arnold. [*Surprised at her significant tone.*] Good gracious me! what's the meaning of all this?

Elizabeth. Well, I don't think there's any object in beating about the bush. I want you to let me go.

Arnold. Go where?

Elizabeth. Away. For always.

Arnold. My dear child, what *are* you talking about?

Elizabeth. I want to be free.

Arnold. [*Amused rather than disconcerted.*] Don't be ridiculous, darling. I daresay you're run down and want a change. I'll take you over to Paris for a fortnight if you like.

Elizabeth. I shouldn't have spoken to you if I hadn't quite made up my mind. We've been married for three years and I don't think it's been a great success. I'm frankly bored by the life you want me to lead.

38

Arnold. Well, if you'll allow me to say so, the fault is yours. We lead a very distinguished, useful life. We know a lot of extremely nice people.

Elizabeth. I'm quite willing to allow that the fault is mine. But how does that make it any better? I'm only twenty-five. If I've made a mistake I have time to correct it.

Arnold. I can't bring myself to take you very seriously.

Elizabeth. You see, I don't love you.

Arnold. Well, I'm awfully sorry. But you weren't obliged to marry me. You've made your bed and I'm afraid you must lie on it.

Elizabeth. That's one of the falsest proverbs in the English language. Why should you lie on the bed you've made if you don't want to? There's always the floor.

Arnold. For goodness' sake don't be funny, Elizabeth.

Elizabeth. I've quite made up my mind to leave you, Arnold.

Arnold. Come, come, Elizabeth, you must be sensible. You haven't any reason to leave me.

Elizabeth. Why should you wish to keep a woman tied to you who wants to be free?

Arnold. I happen to be in love with you.

Elizabeth. You might have said that before.

Arnold. I thought you'd take it for granted. You can't expect a man to go on making love to his wife after three years. I'm very busy. I'm awfully keen on politics and I've worked like a dog to make this house a thing of beauty. After all, a man marries to have a home, but also because he doesn't want to be bothered with sex and all that sort of thing. I fell in love with you the first time I saw you and I've been in love ever since.

Elizabeth. I'm sorry, but if you're not in love with a man his love doesn't mean very much to you.

Arnold. It's so ungrateful. I've done everything in the world for you.

Elizabeth. You've been very kind to me. But you've asked me to lead a life I don't like and that I'm not suited for. I'm awfully sorry to cause you pain, but now you must let me go.

Arnold. Nonsense! I'm a good deal older than you are and I think I have a little more sense. In your interests as well as in mine I'm not going to do anything of the sort.

Elizabeth. [*With a smile.*] How can you prevent me? You can't keep me under lock and key.

Arnold. Please don't talk to me as if I were a foolish child. You're my wife and you're going to remain my wife.

Elizabeth. What sort of a life do you think we should lead? Do you think there'd be any more happiness for you than for me?

Arnold. But what is it precisely that you suggest?

Elizabeth. Well, I want you to let me divorce you.

Arnold. [*Astounded.*] Me? Thank you very much. Are you under the impression I'm going to sacrifice my career for a whim of yours?

Elizabeth. How will it do that?

Arnold. My seat's wobbly enough as it is. Do you think I'd be able to hold it if I were in a divorce case? Even if it were a put-up job, as most divorces are nowadays, it would damn me.

Elizabeth. It's rather hard on a woman to be divorced.

Arnold. [*With sudden suspicion.*] What do you mean by that? Are you in love with some one?

Elizabeth. Yes.

Elizabeth. Teddie Luton.

[*He is astonished for a moment, then bursts into a laugh.*]

Arnold. My poor child, how can you be so ridiculous? Why, he hasn't a bob. He's a perfectly commonplace young man. It's so absurd I can't even be angry with you.

Elizabeth. I've fallen desperately in love with him, Arnold.

Arnold. Well, you'd better fall desperately out.

Elizabeth. He wants to marry me.

Arnold. I daresay he does. He can go to hell.

Elizabeth. It's no good talking like that.

Arnold. Is he your lover?

Elizabeth. No, certainly not.

Arnold. It shows that he's a mean skunk to take advantage of my hospitality to make love to you.

Elizabeth. He's never even kissed me.

Arnold. I'd try telling that to the horse marines if I were you.

Elizabeth. It's because I wanted to do nothing shabby that I told you straight out how things were.

Arnold. How long have you been thinking of this?

Elizabeth. I've been in love with Teddie ever since I knew him.

Arnold. And you never thought of me at all, I suppose.

Elizabeth. Oh, yes, I did. I was miserable. But I can't help myself. I wish I loved you, but I don't.

Arnold. I recommend you to think very carefully before you do anything foolish.

Elizabeth. I have thought very carefully.

Arnold. By God! I don't know why I don't give you a sound hiding. I'm not sure if that wouldn't be the best thing to bring you to your senses.

Elizabeth. Oh, Arnold, don't take it like that.

Arnold. How do you expect me to take it? You come to me quite calmly and say: "I've had enough of you. We've been married three years and I think I'd like to marry somebody else now. Shall I break up your home? What a bore for you! Do you mind my divorcing you? It'll smash up your career, will it? What a pity!" Oh, no, my girl, I may be a fool, but I'm not a damned fool.

Elizabeth. Teddie is leaving here by the first train to-morrow. I warn you that I mean to join him as soon as he can make the necessary arrangements.

Arnold. Where is he?

Elizabeth. I don't know. I suppose he's in his room.

[Arnold goes to the door and calls.]

Arnold. George!

[For a moment he walks up and down the room impatiently. Elizabeth watches him. The Footman comes in.]

Footman. Yes, sir.

Arnold. Tell Mr. Luton to come here at once.

Elizabeth. Ask Mr. Luton if he wouldn't mind coming here for a moment.

Footman. Very good, madam.

[Exit Footman.]

Elizabeth. What are you going to say to him?

Arnold. That's my business.

Elizabeth. I wouldn't make a scene if I were you.

Arnold. I'm not going to make a scene.

[They wait in silence.]

Why did you insist on my mother coming here?

Elizabeth. It seemed to me rather absurd to take up the attitude that I should be contaminated by her when . . .

Arnold. [*Interrupting.*] When you were proposing to do exactly the same thing. Well, now you've seen her what do you think of her? Do you think it's been a success? Is that the sort of woman a man would like his mother to be?

Elizabeth. I've been ashamed. I've been so sorry. It all seemed dreadful and horrible. This morning I happened to notice a rose in

41

the garden. It was all overblown and bedraggled. It looked like a painted old woman. And I remembered that I'd looked at it a day or two ago. It was lovely then, fresh and blooming and fragrant. It may be hideous now, but that doesn't take away from the beauty it had once. That was real.

Arnold. Poetry, by God! As if this were the moment for poetry!

[Teddie comes in. He has changed into a dinner jacket.]

Teddie. [To Elizabeth.] Did you want me?
Arnold. I sent for you.

[Teddie looks from Arnold to Elizabeth. He sees that something has happened.]

When would it be convenient for you to leave this house?

Teddie. I was proposing to go to-morrow morning. But I can very well go at once if you like.

Arnold. I do like.

Teddie. Very well. Is there anything else you wish to say to me?

Arnold. Do you think it was a very honourable thing to come down here and make love to my wife?

Teddie. No, I don't. I haven't been very happy about it. That's why I wanted to go away.

Arnold. Upon my word you're cool.

Teddie. I'm afraid it's no good saying I'm sorry and that sort of thing. You know what the situation is.

Arnold. Is it true that you want to marry Elizabeth?

Teddie. Yes. I should like to marry her as soon as ever I can.

Arnold. Have you thought of me at all? Has it struck you that you're destroying my home and breaking up my happiness?

Teddie. I don't see how there could be much happiness for you if Elizabeth doesn't care for you.

Arnold. Let me tell you that I refuse to have my home broken up by a twopenny-halfpenny adventurer who takes advantage of a foolish woman. I refuse to allow myself to be divorced. I can't prevent my wife from going off with you if she's determined to make a damned fool of herself, but this I tell you: nothing will induce me to divorce her.

Elizabeth. Arnold, that would be monstrous.

Teddie. We could force you.

Arnold. How?

Teddie. If we went away together openly you'd have to bring an action.

Arnold. Twenty-four hours after you leave this house I shall go down to Brighton with a chorus-girl. And neither you nor I will be able to get a divorce. We've had enough divorces in our family. And now get out, get out, get out!

[*Teddie looks uncertainly at Elizabeth.*]

Elizabeth. [*With a little smile.*] Don't bother about me. I shall be all right.

Arnold. Get out! Get out!

END OF THE SECOND ACT

THE THIRD ACT

The Scene is the same as in the preceding Acts.

It is the night of the same day as that on which takes place the action of the second Act.

Champion-Cheney and Arnold, both in dinner jackets, are discovered. Champion-Cheney is seated. Arnold walks restlessly up and down the room.

C.-C. I think, if you'll follow my advice to the letter, you'll probably work the trick.

Arnold. I don't like it, you know. It's against all my principles.

C.-C. My dear Arnold, we all hope that you have before you a distinguished political career. You can't learn too soon that the most useful thing about a principle is that it can always be sacrificed to expediency.

Arnold. But supposing it doesn't come off? Women are incalculable.

C.-C. Nonsense! Men are romantic. A woman will always sacrifice herself if you give her the opportunity. It is her favourite form of self-indulgence.

Arnold. I never know whether you're a humorist or a cynic, father.

C.-C. I'm neither, my dear boy; I'm merely a very truthful man. But people are so unused to the truth that they're apt to mistake it for a joke or a sneer.

Arnold. [*Irritably.*] It seems so unfair that this should happen to me.

C.-C. Keep your head, my boy, and do what I tell you.

[*Lady Kitty and Elizabeth come in. Lady Kitty is in a gorgeous evening gown.*]

Elizabeth. Where is Lord Porteous?

C.-C. He's on the terrace. He's smoking a cigar. [*Going to window.*] Hughie!

[*Porteous comes in.*]

Porteous. [*With a grunt.*] Yes? Where's Mrs. Shenstone?

Elizabeth. Oh, she had a headache. She's gone to bed.

44

[*When Porteous comes in Lady Kitty with a very haughty air purses her lips and takes up an illustrated paper. Porteous gives her an irritated look, takes another illustrated paper and sits himself down at the other end of the room. They are not on speaking terms.*]

C.-C. Arnold and I have just been down to my cottage.

Elizabeth. I wondered where you'd gone.

C.-C. I came across an old photograph album this afternoon. I meant to bring it along before dinner, but I forgot, so we went and fetched it.

Elizabeth. Oh, do let me see it! I love old photographs.

[*He gives her the album, and she, sitting down, puts it on her knees and begins to turn over the pages. He stands over her. Lady Kitty and Porteous take surreptitious glances at one another.*]

C.-C. I thought it might amuse you to see what pretty women looked like five-and-thirty years ago. That was the day of beautiful women.

Elizabeth. Do you think they were more beautiful then than they are now?

C.-C. Oh, much. Now you see lots of pretty little things, but very few beautiful women.

Elizabeth. Aren't their clothes funny?

C.-C. [*Pointing to a photograph.*] That's Mrs. Langtry.

Elizabeth. She has a lovely nose.

C.-C. She was the most wonderful thing you ever saw. Dowagers used to jump on chairs in order to get a good look at her when she came into a drawing-room. I was riding with her once, and we had to have the gates of the livery stable closed when she was getting on her horse because the crowd was so great.

Elizabeth. And who's that?

C.-C. Lady Lonsdale. That's Lady Dudley.

Elizabeth. This is an actress, isn't it?

C.-C. It is, indeed. Ellen Terry. By George! how I loved that woman!

Elizabeth. [*With a smile.*] Dear Ellen Terry!

C.-C. That's Bwabs. I never saw a smarter man in my life. And Oliver Montagu. Henry Manners with his eye-glass.

Elizabeth. Nice-looking, isn't he? And this?

C.-C. That's Mary Anderson. I wish you could have seen her in "A Winter's Tale." Her beauty just took your breath away. And look!

There's Lady Randolph. Bernal Osborne—the wittiest man I ever knew.

Elizabeth. I think it's too sweet. I love their absurd bustles and those tight sleeves.

C.-C. What figures they had! In those days a woman wasn't supposed to be as thin as a rail and as flat as a pancake.

Elizabeth. Oh, but aren't they laced in? How could they bear it?

C.-C. They didn't play golf then, and nonsense like that, you know. They hunted, in a tall hat and a long black habit, and they were very gracious and charitable to the poor in the village.

Elizabeth. Did the poor like it?

C.-C. They had a very thin time if they didn't. When they were in London they drove in the Park every afternoon, and they went to ten-course dinners, where they never met anybody they didn't know. And they had their box at the opera when Patti was singing or Madame Albani.

Elizabeth. Oh, what a lovely little thing! Who on earth is that?

C.-C. That?

Elizabeth. She looks so fragile, like a piece of exquisite china, with all those furs on and her face up against her muff, and the snow falling.

C.-C. Yes, there was quite a rage at that time for being taken in an artificial snowstorm.

Elizabeth. What a sweet smile, so roguish and frank, and debonair! Oh, I wish I looked like that! Do tell me who it is!

C.-C. Don't you know?

Elizabeth. No.

C.-C. Why—it's Kitty.

Elizabeth. Lady Kitty! [*To Lady Kitty.*] Oh, my dear, do look! It's too ravishing. [*She takes the album over to her impulsively.*] Why didn't you tell me you looked like that? Everybody must have been in love with you.

[*Lady Kitty takes the album and looks at it. Then she lets it slip from her hands and covers her face with her hands. She is crying.*]

[*In consternation.*] My dear, what's the matter? Oh, what have I done? I'm so sorry.

Lady Kitty. Don't, don't talk to me. Leave me alone. It's stupid of me.

[*Elizabeth looks at her for a moment perplexed, then, turning round, slips her arm in Champion-Cheney's and leads him out on to the terrace.]*

Elizabeth. [*As they are going, in a whisper.*] Did you do that on purpose?

[*Porteous gets up and goes over to Lady Kitty. He puts his hand on her shoulder. They remain thus for a little while.*]

Porteous. I'm afraid I was very rude to you before dinner, Kitty.

Lady Kitty. [*Taking his hand which is on her shoulder.*] It doesn't matter. I'm sure I was very exasperating.

Porteous. I didn't mean what I said, you know.

Lady Kitty. Neither did I.

Porteous. Of course I know that I'd never have been Prime Minister.

Lady Kitty. How can you talk such nonsense, Hughie? No one would have had a chance if you'd remained in politics.

Porteous. I haven't the character.

Lady Kitty. You have more character than anyone I've ever met.

Porteous. Besides, I don't know that I much wanted to be Prime Minister.

Lady Kitty. Oh, but I should have been so proud of you. Of course you'd have been Prime Minister.

Porteous. I'd have given you India, you know. I think it would have been a very popular appointment.

Lady Kitty. I don't care twopence about India. I'd have been quite content with Western Australia.

Porteous. My dear, you don't think I'd have let you bury yourself in Western Australia?

Lady Kitty. Or Barbadoes.

Porteous. Never. It sounds like a cure for flat feet. I'd have kept you in London.

[*He picks up the album and is about to look at the photograph of Lady Kitty. She puts her hand over it.*]

Lady Kitty. No, don't look.

[*He takes her hand away.*]

Porteous. Don't be so silly.

47

Lady Kitty. Isn't it hateful to grow old?

Porteous. You know, you haven't changed much.

Lady Kitty. [*Enchanted.*] Oh, Hughie, how can you talk such nonsense?

Porteous. Of course you're a little more mature, but that's all. A woman's all the better for being rather mature.

Lady Kitty. Do you really think that?

Porteous. Upon my soul I do.

Lady Kitty. You're not saying it just to please me?

Porteous. No, no.

Lady Kitty. Let me look at the photograph again.

[*She takes the album and looks at the photograph complacently.*]

The fact is, if your bones are good, age doesn't really matter. You'll always be beautiful.

Porteous. [*With a little smile, almost as if he were talking to a child.*] It was silly of you to cry.

Lady Kitty. It hasn't made my eyelashes run, has it?

Porteous. Not a bit.

Lady Kitty. It's very good stuff I use now. They don't stick together either.

Porteous. Look here, Kitty, how much longer do you want to stay here?

Lady Kitty. Oh, I'm quite ready to go whenever you like.

Porteous. Clive gets on my nerves. I don't like the way he keeps hanging about you.

Lady Kitty. [*Surprised, rather amused, and delighted.*] Hughie, you don't mean to say you're jealous of poor Clive?

Porteous. Of course I'm not jealous of him, but he does look at you in a way that I can't help thinking rather objectionable.

Lady Kitty. Hughie, you may throw me downstairs like Amy Robsart; you may drag me about the floor by the hair of my head; I don't care, you're jealous. I shall never grow old.

Porteous. Damn it all, the man was your husband.

Lady Kitty. My dear Hughie, he never had your style. Why, the moment you come into a room everyone looks and says: "Who the devil is that?"

Porteous. What? You think that, do you? Well, I daresay there's something in what you say. These damned Radicals can say what they like, but, by God, Kitty! when a man's a gentleman—well, damn it all, you know what I mean.

Lady Kitty. I think Clive has degenerated dreadfully since we left him.

Porteous. What do you say to making a bee-line for Italy and going to San Michele?

Lady Kitty. Oh, Hughie! It's years since we were there.

Porteous. Wouldn't you like to see it again—just once more?

Lady Kitty. Do you remember the first time we went? It was the most heavenly place I'd ever seen. We'd only left England a month, and I said I'd like to spend all my life there.

Porteous. Of course I remember. And in a fortnight it was yours, lock, stock and barrel.

Lady Kitty. We were very happy there, Hughie.

Porteous. Let's go back once more.

Lady Kitty. I daren't. It must be all peopled with the ghosts of our past. One should never go again to a place where one has been happy. It would break my heart.

Porteous. Do you remember how we used to sit on the terrace of the old castle and look at the Adriatic? We might have been the only people in the world, you and I, Kitty.

Lady Kitty. [*Tragically.*] And we thought our love would last for ever.

[Enter Champion-Cheney.]

Porteous. Is there any chance of bridge this evening?

C.-C. I don't think we can make up a four.

Porteous. What a nuisance that boy went away like that! He wasn't a bad player.

C.-C. Teddie Luton?

Lady Kitty. I think it was very funny his going without saying good-bye to anyone.

C.-C. The young men of the present day are very casual.

Porteous. I thought there was no train in the evening.

C.-C. There isn't. The last train leaves at 5.45.

Porteous. How did he go then?

C.-C. He went.

Porteous. Damned selfish I call it.

Lady Kitty. [*Intrigued.*] Why did he go, Clive?

[Champion-Cheney looks at her for a moment reflectively.]

C.-C. I have something very grave to say to you. Elizabeth wants to leave Arnold.

Lady Kitty. Clive! What on earth for?

C.-C. She's in love with Teddie Luton. That's why he went. The men of my family are really very unfortunate.

49

Porteous. Does she want to run away with him?

Lady Kitty. [*With consternation.*] My dear, what's to be done?

C.-C. I think you can do a great deal.

Lady Kitty. I? What?

C.-C. Tell her, tell her what it means.

[*He looks at her fixedly. She stares at him.*]

Lady Kitty. Oh, no, no!

C.-C. She's a child. Not for Arnold's sake. For her sake. You must.

Lady Kitty. You don't know what you're asking.

C.-C. Yes, I do.

Lady Kitty. Hughie, what shall I do?

Porteous. Do what you like. I shall never blame you for anything.

[*The Footman comes in with a letter on a salver. He hesitates on seeing that Elizabeth is not in the room.*]

C.-C. What is it?

Footman. I was looking for Mrs. Champion-Cheney, sir.

C.-C. She's not here. Is that a letter?

Footman. Yes, sir. It's just been sent up from the "Champion Arms."

C.-C. Leave it. I'll give it to Mrs. Cheney.

Footman. Very good, sir.

[*He brings the tray to Clive, who takes the letter. The Footman goes out.*]

Porteous. Is the "Champion Arms" the local pub?

C.-C. [*Looking at the letter.*] It's by way of being a hotel, but I never heard of anyone staying there.

Lady Kitty. If there was no train I suppose he had to go there.

C.-C. Great minds. I wonder what he has to write about! [*He goes to the door leading on to the garden.*] Elizabeth!

Elizabeth. [*Outside.*] Yes.

C.-C. Here's a note for you.

[*There is silence. They wait for Elizabeth to come. She enters.*]

Elizabeth. It's lovely in the garden to-night.

C.-C. They've just sent this up from the "Champion Arms."

50

Elizabeth. Thank you.

[*Without embarrassment she opens the letter. They watch her while she reads it. It covers three pages. She puts it away in her bag.*]

Lady Kitty. Hughie, I wish you'd fetch me a cloak. I'd like to take a little stroll in the garden, but after thirty years in Italy I find these English summers rather chilly.

[*Without a word Porteous goes out. Elizabeth is lost in thought.*]

I want to talk to Elizabeth, Clive.
C.-C. I'll leave you.

[*He goes out.*]

Lady Kitty. What does he say?
Elizabeth. Who?
Lady Kitty. Mr. Luton.
Elizabeth. [*Gives a little start. Then she looks at Lady Kitty.*] They've told you?
Elizabeth. I don't expect you to have much sympathy for me. Arnold is your son.
Lady Kitty. So pitifully little.
Elizabeth. I'm not suited for this sort of existence. Arnold wants me to take what he calls my place in Society. Oh, I get so bored with those parties in London. All those middle-aged painted women, in beautiful clothes, lolloping round ball-rooms with rather old young men. And the endless luncheons where they gossip about so-and-so's love affairs.
Lady Kitty. Are you very much in love with Mr. Luton?
Elizabeth. I love him with all my heart.
Lady Kitty. And he?
Elizabeth. He's never cared for anyone but me. He never will.
Lady Kitty. Will Arnold let you divorce him?
Elizabeth. No, he won't hear of it. He refuses even to divorce me.
Lady Kitty. Why?
Elizabeth. He thinks a scandal will revive all the old gossip.
Lady Kitty. Oh, my poor child!
Elizabeth. It can't be helped. I'm quite willing to accept the consequences.
Lady Kitty. You don't know what it is to have a man tied to

51

you only by his honour. When married people don't get on they can separate, but if they're not married it's impossible. It's a tie that only death can sever.

Elizabeth. If Teddie stopped caring for me I shouldn't want him to stay with me for five minutes.

Lady Kitty. One says that when one's sure of a man's love, but when one isn't any more—oh, it's so different. In those circumstances one's got to keep a man's love. It's the only thing one has.

Elizabeth. I'm a human being. I can stand on my own feet.

Lady Kitty. Have you any money of your own?

Elizabeth. None.

Lady Kitty. Then how can you stand on your own feet? You think I'm a silly, frivolous woman, but I've learned something in a bitter school. They can make what laws they like, they can give us the suffrage, but when you come down to bedrock it's the man who pays the piper who calls the tune. Woman will only be the equal of man when she earns her living in the same way that he does.

Elizabeth. [*Smiling.*] It sounds rather funny to hear you talk like that.

Lady Kitty. A cook who marries a butler can snap her fingers in his face because she can earn just as much as he can. But a woman in your position and a woman in mine will always be dependent on the men who keep them.

Elizabeth. I don't want luxury. You don't know how sick I am of all this beautiful furniture. These over-decorated houses are like a prison in which I can't breathe. When I drive about in a Callot frock and a Rolls-Royce I envy the shop-girl in a coat and skirt whom I see jumping on the tailboard of a bus.

Lady Kitty. You mean that if need be you could earn your own living?

Elizabeth. Yes.

Lady Kitty. What could you be? A nurse or a typist. It's nonsense. Luxury saps a woman's nerve. And when she's known it once it becomes a necessity.

Elizabeth. That depends on the woman.

Lady Kitty. When we're young we think we're different from everyone else, but when we grow a little older we discover we're all very much of a muchness.

Elizabeth. You're very kind to take so much trouble about me.

Lady Kitty. It breaks my heart to think that you're going to make the same pitiful mistake that I made.

Elizabeth. Oh, don't say it was that, don't, don't.

Lady Kitty. Look at me, Elizabeth, and look at Hughie. Do you think it's been a success? If I had my time over again do you think I'd do it again? Do you think he would?

Elizabeth. You see, you don't know how much I love Teddie.

Lady Kitty. And do you think I didn't love Hughie? Do you think he didn't love me?

Elizabeth. I'm sure he did.

Lady Kitty. Oh, of course in the beginning it was heavenly. We felt so brave and adventurous and we were so much in love. The first two years were wonderful. People cut me, you know, but I didn't mind. I thought love was everything. It *is* a little uncomfortable when you come upon an old friend and go towards her eagerly, so glad to see her, and are met with an icy stare.

Elizabeth. Do you think friends like that are worth having?

Lady Kitty. Perhaps they're not very sure of themselves. Perhaps they're honestly shocked. It's a test one had better not put one's friends to if one can help it. It's rather bitter to find how few one has.

Elizabeth. But one has some.

Lady Kitty. Yes, they ask you to come and see them when they're quite certain no one will be there who might object to meeting you. Or else they say to you: "My dear, you know I'm devoted to you, and I wouldn't mind at all, but my girl's growing up—I'm sure you understand; you won't think it unkind of me if I don't ask you to the house?"

Elizabeth. [*Smiling.*] That doesn't seem to me very serious.

Lady Kitty. At first I thought it rather a relief, because it threw Hughie and me together more. But you know, men are very funny. Even when they are in love they're not in love all day long. They want change and recreation.

Elizabeth. I'm not inclined to blame them for that, poor dears.

Lady Kitty. Then we settled in Florence. And because we couldn't get the society we'd been used to we became used to the society we could get. Loose women and vicious men. Snobs who liked to patronise people with a handle to their names. Vague Italian Princes who were glad to borrow a few francs from Hughie and seedy countesses who liked to drive with me in the Cascine. And then Hughie began to hanker after his old life. He wanted to go big game shooting, but I dared not let him go. I was afraid he'd never come back.

Elizabeth. But you knew he loved you.

Lady Kitty. Oh, my dear, what a blessed institution marriage is—for women, and what fools they are to meddle with it! The Church is so wise to take its stand on the indi—indi—

Elizabeth. Solu—

Lady Kitty. Bility of marriage. Believe me, it's no joke when you have to rely only on yourself to keep a man. I could never afford to grow old. My dear, I'll tell you a secret that I've never told a living soul.

Elizabeth. What is that?

Lady Kitty. My hair is not naturally this colour.

Elizabeth. Really.

Lady Kitty. I touch it up. You would never have guessed, would you?

Elizabeth. Never.

Lady Kitty. Nobody does. My dear, it's white, prematurely of course, but white. I always think it's a symbol of my life. Are you interested in symbolism? I think it's too wonderful.

Elizabeth. I don't think I know very much about it.

Lady Kitty. However tired I've been I've had to be brilliant and gay. I've never let Hughie see the aching heart behind my smiling eyes.

Elizabeth. [*Amused and touched.*] You poor dear.

Lady Kitty. And when I saw he was attracted by some one else the fear and the jealousy that seized me! You see, I didn't dare make a scene as I should have done if I'd been married—I had to pretend not to notice.

Elizabeth. [*Taken aback.*] But do you mean to say he fell in love with anyone else?

Lady Kitty. Of course he did eventually.

Elizabeth. [*Hardly knowing what to say.*] You must have been very unhappy.

Lady Kitty. Oh, I was, dreadfully. Night after night I sobbed my heart out when Hughie told me he was going to play cards at the club and I knew he was with that odious woman. Of course, it wasn't as if there weren't plenty of men who were only too anxious to console me. Men have always been attracted by me, you know.

Elizabeth. Oh, of course, I can quite understand it.

Lady Kitty. But I had my self-respect to think of. I felt that whatever Hughie did I would do nothing that I should regret.

Elizabeth. You must be very glad now.

Lady Kitty. Oh, yes. Notwithstanding all my temptations I've been absolutely faithful to Hughie in spirit.

Elizabeth. I don't think I quite understand what you mean.

Lady Kitty. Well, there was a poor Italian boy, young Count Castel Giovanni, who was so desperately in love with me that his mother begged me not to be too cruel. She was afraid he'd go into a consumption. What could I do? And then, oh, years later, there was

Antonio Melita. He said he'd shoot himself unless I—well, you understand I couldn't let the poor boy shoot himself.

Elizabeth. D'you think he really would have shot himself?

Lady Kitty. Oh, one never knows, you know. Those Italians are so passionate. He was really rather a lamb. He had such beautiful eyes.

[Elizabeth looks at her for a long time and a certain horror seizes her of this dissolute, painted old woman.]

Elizabeth. [*Hoarsely.*] Oh, but I think that's—dreadful.

Lady Kitty. Are you shocked? One sacrifices one's life for love and then one finds that love doesn't last. The tragedy of love isn't death or separation. One gets over them. The tragedy of love is indifference.

[Arnold comes in.]

Arnold. Can I have a little talk with you, Elizabeth?

Elizabeth. Of course.

Arnold. Shall we go for a stroll in the garden?

Elizabeth. If you like.

Lady Kitty. No, stay here. I'm going out anyway.

[Exit Lady Kitty.]

Arnold. I want you to listen to me for a few minutes, Elizabeth. I was so taken aback by what you told me just now that I lost my head. I was rather absurd and I beg your pardon. I said things I regret.

Elizabeth. Oh, don't blame yourself. I'm sorry that I should have given you occasion to say them.

Arnold. I want to ask you if you've quite made up your mind to go.

Elizabeth. Quite.

Arnold. Just now I seem to have said all that I didn't want to say and nothing that I did. I'm stupid and tongue-tied. I never told you how deeply I loved you.

Elizabeth. Oh, Arnold!

Arnold. Please let me speak now. It's so very difficult. If I seemed absorbed in politics and the house, and so on, to the exclusion of my interest in you, I'm dreadfully sorry. I suppose it was absurd of me to think you would take my great love for granted.

Elizabeth. But, Arnold, I'm not reproaching you.

Arnold. I'm reproaching myself. I've been tactless and neglectful. But I do ask you to believe that it hasn't been because I didn't love you. Can you forgive me?

Elizabeth. I don't think that there's anything to forgive.

Arnold. It wasn't till to-day when you talked of leaving me that I realised how desperately in love with you I was.

Elizabeth. After three years?

Arnold. I'm so proud of you. I admire you so much. When I see you at a party, so fresh and lovely, and everybody wondering at you, I have a sort of little thrill because you're mine, and afterwards I shall take you home.

Elizabeth. Oh, Arnold, you're exaggerating.

Arnold. I can't imagine this house without you. Life seems on a sudden all empty and meaningless. Oh, Elizabeth, don't you love me at all?

Elizabeth. It's much better to be honest. No.

Arnold. Doesn't my love mean anything to you?

Elizabeth. I'm very grateful to you. I'm sorry to cause you pain. What would be the good of my staying with you when I should be wretched all the time?

Arnold. Do you love that man as much as all that? Does my unhappiness mean nothing to you?

Elizabeth. Of course it does. It breaks my heart. You see, I never knew I meant so much to you. I'm so touched. And I'm so sorry, Arnold, really sorry. But I can't help myself.

Arnold. Poor child, it's cruel of me to torture you.

Elizabeth. Oh, Arnold, believe me, I have tried to make the best of it. I've tried to love you, but I can't. After all, one either loves or one doesn't. Trying is no help. And now I'm at the end of my tether. I can't help the consequences—I must do what my whole self yearns for.

Arnold. My poor child, I'm so afraid you'll be unhappy. I'm so afraid you'll regret.

Elizabeth. You must leave me to my fate. I hope you'll forget me and all the unhappiness I've caused you.

Arnold. [*There is a pause. Arnold walks up and down the room reflectively. He stops and faces her.*] If you love this man and want to go to him I'll do nothing to prevent you. My only wish is to do what is best for you.

Elizabeth. Arnold, that's awfully kind of you. If I'm treating you badly at least I want you to know that I'm grateful for all your kindness to me.

Arnold. But there's one favour I should like you to do me. Will you?

Elizabeth. Oh, Arnold, of course I'll do anything I can.

Arnold. Teddie hasn't very much money. You've been used to a certain amount of luxury, and I can't bear to think that you should do without anything you've had. It would kill me to think that you were suffering any hardship or privation.

Elizabeth. Oh, but Teddie can earn enough for our needs. After all, we don't want much money.

Arnold. I'm afraid my mother's life hasn't been very easy, but it's obvious that the only thing that's made it possible is that Porteous was rich. I want you to let me make you an allowance of two thousand a year.

Elizabeth. Oh, no, I couldn't think of it. It's absurd.

Arnold. I beg you to accept it. You don't know what a difference it will make.

Elizabeth. It's awfully kind of you, Arnold. It humiliates me to speak about it. Nothing would induce me to take a penny from you.

Arnold. Well, you can't prevent me from opening an account at my bank in your name. The money shall be paid in every quarter whether you touch it or not, and if you happen to want it, it will be there waiting for you.

Elizabeth. You overwhelm me, Arnold. There's only one thing I want you to do for me. I should be very grateful if you would divorce me as soon as you possibly can.

Arnold. No, I won't do that. But I'll give you cause to divorce me.

Elizabeth. You!

Arnold. Yes. But of course you'll have to be very careful for a bit. I'll put it through as quickly as possible, but I'm afraid you can't hope to be free for over six months.

Elizabeth. But, Arnold, your seat and your political career!

Arnold. Oh, well, my father gave up his seat under similar circumstances. He's got along very comfortably without politics.

Elizabeth. But they're your whole life.

Arnold. After all one can't have it both ways. You can't serve God and Mammon. If you want to do the decent thing you have to be prepared to suffer for it.

Elizabeth. But I don't want you to suffer for it.

Arnold. At first I rather hesitated at the scandal. But I daresay that was only weakness on my part. Under the circumstances I should have liked to keep out of the Divorce Court if I could.

Elizabeth. Arnold, you're making me absolutely miserable.

Arnold. What you said before dinner was quite right. It's nothing for a man, but it makes so much difference to a woman. Naturally I must think of you first.

Elizabeth. That's absurd. It's out of the question. Whatever there's to pay I must pay it.

Arnold. It's not very much I'm asking you, Elizabeth.

Elizabeth. I'm taking everything from you.

Arnold. It's the only condition I make. My mind is absolutely made up. I will never divorce you, but I will enable you to divorce me.

Elizabeth. Oh, Arnold, it's cruel to be so generous.

Arnold. It's not generous at all. It's the only way I have of showing you how deep and passionate and sincere my love is for you.

[There is a silence. He holds out his hand.]

Good-night. I have a great deal of work to do before I go to bed.

Elizabeth. Good-night.

Arnold. Do you mind if I kiss you?

Elizabeth. [*With agony.*] Oh, Arnold!

[He gravely kisses her on the forehead and then goes out. Elizabeth stands lost in thought. She is shattered. Lady Kitty and Porteous come in. Lady Kitty wears a cloak.]

Lady Kitty. You're alone, Elizabeth?

Elizabeth. That note you asked me about, Lady Kitty, from Teddie . . .

Lady Kitty. Yes?

Elizabeth. He wanted to have a talk with me before he went away. He's waiting for me in the summer house by the tennis court. Would Lord Porteous mind going down and asking him to come here?

Porteous. Certainly. Certainly.

Elizabeth. Forgive me for troubling you. But it's very important.

Porteous. No trouble at all.

[He goes out.]

Lady Kitty. Hughie and I will leave you alone.

Elizabeth. But I don't want to be left alone. I want you to stay.

Lady Kitty. What are you going to say to him?

Elizabeth. [*Desperately.*] Please don't ask me questions. I'm so frightfully unhappy.

58

Lady Kitty. My poor child!

Elizabeth. Oh, isn't life rotten? Why can't one be happy without making other people unhappy?

Lady Kitty. I wish I knew how to help you. I'm simply devoted to you. [*She hunts about in her mind for something to do or say.*] Would you like my lip-stick?

Elizabeth. [*Smiling through her tears.*] Thanks. I never use one.

Lady Kitty. Oh, but just try. It's such a comfort when you're in trouble.

[Enter Porteous and Teddie.]

Porteous. I brought him. He said he'd be damned if he'd come.

Lady Kitty. When a lady sent for him? Are these the manners of the young men of to-day?

Teddie. When you've been solemnly kicked out of a house once I think it seems rather pushing to come back again as though nothing had happened.

Elizabeth. Teddie, I want you to be serious.

Teddie. Darling, I had such a rotten dinner at that pub. If you ask me to be serious on the top of that I shall cry.

Elizabeth. Don't be idiotic, Teddie. [*Her voice faltering.*] I'm so utterly wretched.

[He looks at her for a moment gravely.]

Teddie. What is it?

Elizabeth. I can't come away with you, Teddie.

Teddie. Why not?

Elizabeth. [*Looking away in embarrassment.*] I don't love you enough.

Teddie. Fiddle!

Elizabeth. [*With a flash of anger.*] Don't say "Fiddle" to me.

Teddie. I shall say exactly what I like to you.

Elizabeth. I won't be bullied.

Teddie. Now look here, Elizabeth, you know perfectly well that I'm in love with you, and I know perfectly well that you're in love with me. So what are you talking nonsense for?

Elizabeth. [*Her voice breaking.*] I can't say it if you're cross with me.

Teddie. [*Smiling very tenderly.*] I'm not cross with you, silly.

Elizabeth. It's harder still when you're being rather an owl.

Teddie. [*With a chuckle.*] Am I mistaken in thinking you're not very easy to please?

Elizabeth. Oh, it's monstrous. I was all wrought up and ready to do anything, and now you've thoroughly put me out. I feel like a great big fat balloon that some one has put a long pin into. [*With a sudden look at him.*] Have you done it on purpose?

Teddie. Upon my soul I don't know what you're talking about.

Elizabeth. I wonder if you're really much cleverer than I think you are.

Teddie. [*Taking her hands and making her sit down.*] Now tell me exactly what you want to say. By the way, do you want Lady Kitty and Lord Porteous to be here?

Elizabeth. Yes.

Lady Kitty. Elizabeth asked us to stay.

Teddie. Oh, I don't mind, bless you. I only thought you might feel rather in the way.

Lady Kitty. [*Frigidly.*] A gentlewoman never feels in the way, Mr. Luton.

Teddie. Won't you call me Teddie? Everybody does, you know.

[*Lady Kitty tries to give him a withering look, but she finds it very difficult to prevent herself from smiling. Teddie strokes Elizabeth's hands. She draws them away.*]

Elizabeth. No, don't do that. Teddie, it wasn't true when I said I didn't love you. Of course I love you. But Arnold loves me, too. I didn't know how much.

Teddie. What has he been saying to you?

Elizabeth. He's been very good to me, and so kind. I didn't know he could be so kind. He offered to let me divorce him.

Teddie. That's very decent of him.

Elizabeth. But don't you see, it ties my hands. How can I accept such a sacrifice? I should never forgive myself if I profited by his generosity.

Teddie. If another man and I were devilish hungry and there was only one mutton chop between us, and he said, "You eat it," I wouldn't waste a lot of time arguing. I'd wolf it before he changed his mind.

Elizabeth. Don't talk like that. It maddens me. I'm trying to do the right thing.

Teddie. You're not in love with Arnold; you're in love with me. It's idiotic to sacrifice your life for a slushy sentiment.

Elizabeth. After all, I did marry him.

Teddie. Well, you made a mistake. A marriage without love is no marriage at all.

Elizabeth. *I* made the mistake. Why should he suffer for it? If anyone has to suffer it's only right that I should.

Teddie. What sort of a life do you think it would be with him? When two people are married it's very difficult for one of them to be unhappy without making the other unhappy too.

Elizabeth. I can't take advantage of his generosity.

Teddie. I daresay he'll get a lot of satisfaction out of it.

Elizabeth. You're being beastly, Teddie. He was simply wonderful. I never knew he had it in him. He was really noble.

Teddie. You are talking rot, Elizabeth.

Elizabeth. I wonder if you'd be capable of acting like that.

Teddie. Acting like what?

Elizabeth. What would you do if I were married to you and came and told you I loved somebody else and wanted to leave you?

Teddie. You have very pretty blue eyes, Elizabeth. I'd black first one and then the other. And after that we'd see.

Elizabeth. You damned brute!

Teddie. I've often thought I wasn't quite a gentleman. Had it ever struck you?

[They look at one another for a while.]

Elizabeth. You know, you are taking an unfair advantage of me. I feel as if I came to you quite unsuspectingly and when I wasn't looking you kicked me on the shins.

Teddie. Don't you think we'd get on rather well together?

Porteous. Elizabeth's a fool if she don't stick to her husband. It's bad enough for the man, but for the woman—it's damnable. I hold no brief for Arnold. He plays bridge like a foot. Saving your presence, Kitty, I think he's a prig.

Lady Kitty. Poor dear, his father was at his age. I daresay he'll grow out of it.

Porteous. But you stick to him, Elizabeth, stick to him. Man is a gregarious animal. We're members of a herd. If we break the herd's laws we suffer for it. And we suffer damnably.

Lady Kitty. Oh, Elizabeth, my dear child, don't go. It's not worth it. It's not worth it. I tell you that, and I've sacrificed everything to love.

[A pause.]

Elizabeth. I'm afraid.

61

Teddie. [*In a whisper.*] Elizabeth.

Elizabeth. I can't face it. It's asking too much of me. Let's say good-bye to one another, Teddie. It's the only thing to do. And have pity on me. I'm giving up all my hope of happiness.

[*He goes up to her and looks into her eyes.*]

Teddie. But I wasn't offering you happiness. I don't think my sort of love tends to happiness. I'm jealous. I'm not a very easy man to get on with. I'm often out of temper and irritable. I should be fed to the teeth with you sometimes, and so would you be with me. I daresay we'd fight like cat and dog, and sometimes we'd hate each other. Often you'd be wretched and bored stiff and lonely, and often you'd be frightfully homesick, and then you'd regret all you'd lost. Stupid women would be rude to you because we'd run away together. And some of them would cut you. I don't offer you peace and quietness. I offer you unrest and anxiety. I don't offer you happiness. I offer you love.

Elizabeth. [*Stretching out her arms.*] You hateful creature, I absolutely adore you!

[*He throws his arms round her and kisses her passionately on the lips.*]

Lady Kitty. Of course the moment he said he'd give her a black eye I knew it was finished.

Porteous. [*Good-humouredly.*] You are a fool, Kitty.

Lady Kitty. I know I am, but I can't help it.

Teddie. Let's make a bolt for it now.

Elizabeth. Shall we?

Teddie. This minute.

Porteous. You're damned fools, both of you, damned fools! If you like you can have my car.

Teddie. That's awfully kind of you. As a matter of fact I got it out of the garage. It's just along the drive.

Porteous. [*Indignantly.*] How do you mean, you got it out of the garage?

Teddie. Well, I thought there'd be a lot of bother, and it seemed to me the best thing would be for Elizabeth and me not to stand upon the order of our going, you know. Do it now. An excellent motto for a business man.

Porteous. Do you mean to say you were going to steal my car?

Teddie. Not exactly. I was only going to bolshevise it, so to speak.

Porteous. I'm speechless. I'm absolutely speechless.

Teddie. Hang it all, I couldn't carry Elizabeth all the way to London. She's so damned plump.

Elizabeth. You dirty dog!

Porteous. [*Spluttering.*] Well, well, well! . . . [*Helplessly.*] I like him, Kitty, it's no good pretending I don't. I like him.

Teddie. The moon's shining, Elizabeth. We'll drive all through the night.

Porteous. They'd better go to San Michele. I'll wire to have it got ready for them.

Lady Kitty. That's where we went when Hughie and I . . . [*Faltering.*] Oh, you dear things, how I envy you!

Porteous. [*Mopping his eyes.*] Now don't cry, Kitty. Confound you, don't cry.

Teddie. Come, darling.

Elizabeth. But I can't go like this.

Teddie. Nonsense! Lady Kitty will lend you her cloak. Won't you?

Lady Kitty. [*Taking it off.*] You're capable of tearing it off my back if I don't.

Teddie. [*Putting the cloak on Elizabeth.*] And we'll buy you a tooth-brush in London in the morning.

Lady Kitty. She must write a note for Arnold. I'll put it on her pincushion.

Teddie. Pincushion be blowed! Come, darling. We'll drive through the dawn and through the sunrise.

Elizabeth. [*Kissing Lady Kitty and Porteous.*] Good-bye. Good-bye.

[Teddie stretches out his hand and she takes it. Hand in hand they go out into the night.]

Lady Kitty. Oh, Hughie, how it all comes back to me! Will they suffer all we suffered? And have we suffered all in vain?

Porteous. My dear, I don't know that in life it matters so much what you do as what you are. No one can learn by the experience of another because no circumstances are quite the same. If we made rather a hash of things perhaps it was because we were rather trivial people. You can do anything in this world if you're prepared to take the consequences, and consequences depend on character.

[Enter Champion-Cheney, rubbing his hands. He is as pleased as Punch.]

C.-C. Well, I think I've settled the hash of that young man.

Lady Kitty. Oh!

C.-C. You have to get up very early in the morning to get the better of your humble servant.

[There is the sound of a car starting.]

Lady Kitty. What is that?

C.-C. It sounds like a car. I expect it's your chauffeur taking one of the maids for a joy-ride.

Porteous. Whose hash are you talking about?

C.-C. Mr. Edward Luton's, my dear Hughie. I told Arnold exactly what to do and he's done it. What makes a prison? Why, bars and bolts. Remove them and a prisoner won't want to escape. Clever, I flatter myself.

Porteous. You were always that, Clive, but at the moment you're obscure.

C.-C. I told Arnold to go to Elizabeth and tell her she could have her freedom. I told him to sacrifice himself all along the line. I know what women are. The moment every obstacle was removed to her marriage with Teddie Luton, half the allurement was gone.

Lady Kitty. Arnold did that?

C.-C. He followed my instructions to the letter. I've just seen him. She's shaken. I'm willing to bet five hundred pounds to a penny that she won't bolt. A downy old bird, eh? Downy's the word. Downy.

[He begins to laugh. They laugh, too. Presently they are all three in fits of laughter.]

[The Curtain Falls]

THE END

EAST OF SUEZ

DRAMATIS PERSONÆ

Daisy
George Conway
Henry Anderson
Harold Knox
Lee Tai Cheng
Sylvia Knox
Amah
Wu

The action of the play takes place in Peking

SCENE I

A street in Peking

Several shops are shown. Their fronts are richly decorated with carved wood painted red and profusely gilt. The counters are elaborately carved. Outside are huge sign-boards. The shops are open to the street and you can see the various wares they sell. One is a coffin shop, where the coolies are at work on a coffin: other coffins, ready for sale, are displayed; some of them are of plain deal, others are rich, with black and gold. The next shop is a money changer's. Then there is a lantern shop in which all manner of coloured lanterns are hanging. After this comes a druggist where there are queer things in bottles and dried herbs. A small stuffed crocodile is a prominent object. Next to this is a shop where crockery is sold, large coloured jars, plates, and all manner of strange animals. In all the shops two or three Chinamen are seated. Some read newspapers through great horn spectacles; some smoke water pipes.

The street is crowded. Here is an itinerant cook with his two chests, in one of which is burning charcoal: he serves out bowls of rice and condiments to the passers-by who want food. There is a barber with the utensils of his trade. A coolie, seated on a stool, is having his head shaved. Chinese walk to and fro.

Some are coolies and wear blue cotton in various stages of raggedness; some in black gowns and caps and black shoes are merchants and clerks. There is a beggar, gaunt and thin, with an untidy mop of bristly hair, in tatters of indescribable filthiness. He stops at one of the shops and begins a long wail. For a time no one takes any notice of him, but presently on a word from the fat shopkeeper an assistant gives him a few cash and he wanders on. Coolies, half naked, hurry by, bearing great bales on their yokes. They utter little sharp cries for people to get out of their way. Peking carts with their blue hoods rumble noisily along. Rickshaws pass rapidly in both directions, and the rickshaw boys shout for the crowd to make way. In the rickshaws are grave Chinese. Some are dressed in white ducks after the European fashion; in other rickshaws are Chinese women in long smocks and wide trousers or Manchu ladies, with their faces painted like masks, in embroidered silks. Women of various sorts stroll about the street or enter the shops. You see them chaffering for various articles.

A water-carrier passes along with a creaking barrow, slopping the water as he goes; an old blind woman, a masseuse, advances slowly, striking wooden clappers to proclaim her calling. A musician stands on the curb and plays a tuneless melody on a one-stringed fiddle. From the distance comes the muffled sound of gongs. There is a babel of sound caused by the talking of all these people, by the cries of coolies, the gong, the clappers, and the fiddle. From burning joss-sticks in the shops in front of the household god comes a savour of incense.

A couple of Mongols ride across on shaggy ponies; they wear high boots and Astrakhan caps. Then a string of camels sways slowly down the street. They carry great burdens of skins from the deserts of Mongolia. They are accompanied by wild looking fellows. Two stout Chinese gentlemen are giving their pet birds an airing; the birds are attached by the leg with a string and sit on little wooden perches. The two Chinese gentlemen discuss their merits. Round about them small boys play. They run hither and thither pursuing one another amid the crowd.

END OF SCENE I

SCENE II

A small verandah on an upper storey of the British American Tobacco Company's premises, the upper part of which the staff lives in. At the back are heavy arches of whitewashed masonry and a low wall which serves as a parapet. Green blinds are drawn. There is a bamboo table on which are copies of illustrated papers. A couple of long bamboo chairs and two or three smaller arm chairs. The floor is tiled.

On one of the long chairs Harold Knox is lying asleep. He is a young man of pleasing appearance. He wears white ducks, but he has taken off his coat, which lies on a chair, and his collar and tie and pin. They are on the table by his side. He is troubled by a fly and, half waking but with his eyes still closed, tries to drive it away.

Knox. Curse it. [*He opens his eyes and yawns.*] Boy!
Wu. [*Outside.*] Ye.
Knox. What's the time?

[Wu comes in; he is a Chinese servant in a long white gown with a black cap on his head. He bears a tray on which is a bottle of whisky, a glass and a syphon.]

Wu. My no sabe.
Knox. Anyhow it's time for a whisky and soda. [Wu *puts the tray down on the table.* Knox *smiles.*] Intelligent anticipation. Model servant and all that sort of thing. [Wu *pours out the whisky.*] You don't care if I drink myself to death, Wu—do you? [Wu *smiles, showing all his teeth.*] Fault of the climate. Give me the glass. [Wu *does so.*] You're like a mother to me, Wu. [*He drinks and puts down the glass.*] By George, I feel another man. The bull-dog breed, Wu. Never say die. Rule Britannia. Pull up the blinds, you lazy blighter. The sun's off and the place is like a oven.

[Wu goes over and pulls up one blind after the other. An expanse of blue sky is seen. Henry Anderson comes in. He is a man of thirty, fair, good-looking, with a pleasant, honest face. His obvious straightforwardness and sincerity make him attractive.]

Harry. [*Breezily.*] Hulloa, Harold, you seem to be taking it easy.

Knox. There was nothing to do in the office and I thought I'd get in my beauty sleep while I had the chance.

Harry. I thought you had your beauty sleep before midnight.

Knox. I'm taking time by the forelock so as to be on the safe side.

Harry. Are you going on the loose again to-night?

Knox. Again, Henry?

Harry. You were blind last night.

Knox. [*With great satisfaction.*] Paralytic.... Hulloa, who's this? [*He catches sight of the* Amah *who has just entered. She is a little, thin, wrinkled, elderly Chinawoman in a long smock and trousers. She has gold pins in her sleek black hair. When she sees she has been noticed she smiles obsequiously.*] Well, fair charmer, what can we do for you?

Harry. What does she want, Wu?

Knox. Is this the face that launched a thousand ships?

Amah. My Missy have pay my letter.

Harry. [*With sudden eager interest.*] Are you Mrs. Rathbone's amah? Have you got a letter for me?

Amah. My belong Missy Rathbone amah.

Harry. Well, hurry up, don't be all night about it. Lend me a dollar, Harold. I want to give it to the old girl.

[*The* Amah *takes a note out of her sleeve and gives it to* Harry. *He opens it and reads.*]

Knox. I haven't got a dollar. Give her a chit or ask Wu. He's the only man I know who's got any money.

Harry. Let me have a dollar, Wu. Chop-chop.

Wu. My go catchee.

[*He goes out. The* Amah *is standing near the table. While* Knox *and* Harry *go on talking she notices* Knox's *pin. She smiles and smiles and makes little bows to the two men, but at the same time her hand cautiously reaches out for the pin and closes on it. Then she secretes it in her sleeve.*]

Harry. I thought you were going to play tennis this afternoon.

Knox. So I am later on.

Harry. [*Smiling.*] Do it now, dear boy. That is a precept a business man should never forget.

Knox. I should hate to think you wanted to be rid of me.

Harry. I dote on your company, but I feel that I mustn't be selfish.

Knox. [*Pulling his leg.*] To tell you the truth I don't feel very fit to-day.

Harry. A little bilious, I dare say. Half a dozen hard sets are just what you want. [*He hands* Knox *his coat.*]

Knox. What is this?

Harry. Your coat.

Knox. You're making yourself almost more distressingly plain than nature has already made you.

[Wu *comes back and hands* Harry *a dollar, and then goes out.* Harry *gives the dollar to the* Amah.]

Harry. Here's a dollar for you, amah. You go back to missy and tell her it's all right and will she come chop-chop. Sabe?

Amah. My sabe. Goo'-bye.

Knox. God bless you, dearie. It's done me good to see your winsome little face.

Harry. [*With a smile.*] Shut up, Harold.

[*The* Amah *with nods, smiles and bows, goes out.*]

Knox. Harry, my poor friend, is it possible that you have an assignation?

Harry. What is possible is that if you don't get out quick I'll throw you out.

Knox. Why didn't you say you were expecting a girl?

Harry. I'm not; I'm expecting a lady.

Knox. Are you sure you know how to behave? If you'd like me to stay and see you don't do the wrong thing I'll chuck my tennis. I'm always ready to sacrifice myself for a friend.

Harry. Has it struck you that the distance from the verandah to the street is very considerable?

Knox. And the pavement is hard. I flatter myself I can take a hint. I wonder where the devil my pin is. I left it on the table.

Harry. I expect Wu put it away.

Knox. It's much more likely that old woman pinched it.

Harry. Oh, nonsense. She wouldn't dream of such a thing. I believe Mrs. Rathbone's had her for ages.

Knox. Who is Mrs. Rathbone?

Harry. [*Not wishing to be questioned.*] A friend of mine.

[George Conway *comes in. He is a tall, dark man in the early thirties. He is a handsome, well-built fellow, of a somewhat rugged appearance, but urbane and self-assured.*]

70

George. May I come in?

Harry. [*Eagerly, shaking him warmly by the hand.*] At last. By Jove, it's good to see you again. You know Knox, don't you?

George. I think so.

Knox. I wash bottles in the B. A. T. I don't expect the legation bloods to be aware of my existence.

George. [*With a twinkle in his eye.*] I don't know that an Assistant Chinese Secretary is such a blood as all that.

Knox. You've just been down to Fuchow, haven't you?

George. Yes, I only got back this morning.

Knox. Did you see Freddy Baker by any chance?

George. Yes, poor chap.

Knox. Oh, I've got no pity for him. He's just a damned fool.

Harry. Why?

Knox. Haven't you heard? He's married a half-caste.

Harry. What of it? I believe she's a very pretty girl.

Knox. I daresay she is. But hang it all, he needn't have married her.

George. I don't think it was a very wise thing to do.

Harry. I should have thought all those prejudices were out of date. Why shouldn't a man marry a half-caste if he wants to?

Knox. It can't be very nice to have a wife whom even the missionary ladies turn up their noses at.

Harry. [*With a shrug of the shoulders.*] You wait till Freddy's number one in Hankow and can entertain. I bet the white ladies will be glad enough to know his missus then.

George. Yes, but that's just it. He'll never get a good job with a Eurasian wife.

Harry. He's in Jardine's, isn't he? Do you mean to say it's going to handicap a man in a shipping firm because he's married a woman who's partly Chinese?

George. Of course it is. Jardine's are about the most important firm in China and the manager of one of their principal branches has definite social obligations. Freddy Baker will be sent to twopenny halfpenny outports where his wife doesn't matter.

Knox. I think he's damned lucky if he's not asked to resign.

Harry. It's cruel. His wife may be a charming and cultivated woman.

Knox. Have you ever known a half-caste that was?

Harry. I have.

Knox. Well, I've been in this country for seven years and I've never met one, male or female, that didn't give me the shivers.

Harry. I've no patience with you. You're a perfect damned fool.

71

Knox. [*A little surprised, but quite good-humoured.*] You're getting rather excited, aren't you?

Harry. [*Hotly.*] I hate injustice.

George. Do you think it really is injustice? The English are not an unkindly race. If they've got a down on half-castes there are probably very good grounds for it.

Harry. What are they?

Knox. We don't much like their morals, but we can't stick their manners.

George. Somehow or other they seem to inherit all the bad qualities of the two races from which they spring and none of the good ones. I'm sure there are exceptions, but on the whole the Eurasian is vulgar and noisy. He can't tell the truth if he tries.

Knox. To do him justice, he seldom tries.

George. He's as vain as a peacock. He'll cringe when he's afraid of you and he'll bully when he's not. You can never rely on him. He's crooked from the crown of his German hat to the toes of his American boots.

Knox. Straight from the shoulder. Take the count, old man.

Harry. [*Frigidly.*] Oughtn't you to be going?

Knox. [*Smiling.*] No, but I will.

Harry. I'm sorry if I was rude to you just now, old man.

Knox. Silly ass, you've broken no bones; my self-esteem, thank God, is unimpaired. [*He goes out.*

Harry. I say, I'm awfully glad you're back, George. You can't think how I miss you when you're away.

George. As soon as the shooting starts we'll try and get two or three days together in the country.

Harry. Yes, that would be jolly. [*Calling.*] Wu.

Wu. [*Outside.*] Ye'.

Harry. Bring tea for three.

George. Who is the third?

Harry. When you said you could come round I asked somebody I want you very much to meet.

George. Who is that?

Harry. Mrs. Rathbone ... I'm going to be married to her and we want you to be our best man.

George. Harry.

Harry. [*Boyishly.*] I thought you'd be surprised.

George. My dear old boy, I am so glad. I hope you'll be awfully happy.

Harry. I'm awfully happy now.

George. Why have you kept it so dark?

Harry. I didn't want to say anything till it was all settled.

Besides, I've only known her six weeks. I met her when I was down in Shanghai....

George. Is she a widow?

Harry. Yes, she was married to an American in the F. M. S.

George. Is she American?

Harry. Only by marriage. I'm afraid she didn't have a very happy married life.

George. Poor thing. I think I'd take a small bet that you won't beat her.

Harry. I mean to try my best to make her happy.

George. You old fool, I've never known a man who was likely to make a better husband.

Harry. I'm most awfully in love with her, George.

George. Isn't that ripping? How old is she?

Harry. Only twenty-two. She's the loveliest thing you ever saw.

George. And is she in love with you?

Harry. She says so.

George. She damned well ought to be.

Harry. I do hope you'll like her, George.

George. Of course I shall. You're not the sort of chap to fall in love with a woman who isn't nice.

[Harry *walks up and down for a moment restlessly.*]

Harry. Will you have a whisky and soda?

George. No, thanks ... I'll wait for tea.

Harry. She ought to be here in a moment. [*Suddenly making up his mind.*] It's no good beating about the bush. I may as well tell you at once. Her—her mother was Chinese.

George. [*Unable to conceal his dismay.*] Oh, Harry. [*A pause.*] I wish I hadn't said all that I did just now.

Harry. Of course you didn't know.

George. [*Gravely.*] I should have had to say something very like it, Harry. But I shouldn't have put it so bluntly.

Harry. You said yourself there were exceptions.

George. I know. [*Distressed.*] Won't your people be rather upset?

Harry. I don't see how it can matter to them. They're nine thousand miles away.

George. Who was her father?

Harry. Oh, he was a merchant. He's dead. And her mother is too.

George. That's something. I don't think you'd much like having a Chinese mother-in-law about the place.

Harry. George, you won't let it make any difference, will you? We've known one another all our lives.

George. My dear old chap, as far as I'm concerned I shouldn't care if you married the first cousin of the Ace of Spades. I don't want you to make a hash of things.

Harry. Wait till you see her. She's the most fascinating thing you ever met.

George. Yes, they can be charming. I was awfully in love with a half—with a Eurasian girl myself years ago. It was before you came out to the country. I wanted to marry her.

Harry. Why didn't you?

George. It was up in Chung-king. I'd just been appointed vice-consul. I was only twenty-three. The Minister wired from Peking that I'd have to resign if I did. I hadn't a bob except my salary and they transferred me to Canton to get me away.

Harry. It's different for you. You're in the service and you may be Minister one of these days. I'm only a merchant.

George. Even for you there'll be difficulties, you know. Has it occurred to you that the white ladies won't be very nice?

Harry. I can do without their society.

George. You must know some people. It means you'll have to hobnob with Eurasian clerks and their wives. I'm afraid you'll find it pretty rotten.

Harry. If you'll stick to me I don't care.

George. I suppose you've absolutely made up your mind?

Harry. Absolutely.

George. In that case I've got nothing more to say. You can't expect me not to be a little disappointed, but after all the chief thing is your happiness, and whatever I can do I will. You can put your shirt on that.

Harry. You're a brick, George.

George. The little lady ought to be here, oughtn't she?

Harry. I think I hear her on the stairs.

[*He goes to the entrance and then out.* Wu *brings in the tea and sets it on the table.* George *walks over to the parapet and looks thoughtfully before him. There is a sound of voices in the adjoining room.*]

Harry. [*Outside.*] Come in; he's on the verandah.

Daisy. [*Outside.*] One brief look in the glass and then I'm ready.

[Harry *enters*.]

Harry. She's just coming.
George. I bet she's powdering her nose.
Daisy. Here I am.

[*Daisy enters. She is an extremely pretty woman, beautifully, perhaps a little showily, dressed. She has a pale, very clear, slightly sallow skin, and beautiful dark eyes. There is only the very faintest suspicion in them of the Chinese slant. Her hair is abundant and black.*]

Harry. This is George Conway, Daisy.

[George *stares at her. At first he is not quite sure that he recognizes her, then suddenly he does, but only the slightest movement of the eyes betrays him.*]

Daisy. How do you do. I told Harry I had an idea I must have met you somewhere. I don't think I have after all.
Harry. George flatters himself he's not easily forgotten.
Daisy. But I've heard so much about you from Harry that I feel as though we were old friends.
George. It's very kind of you to say so.
Harry. Supposing you poured out the tea, Daisy.
George. I'm dying for a cup.

[*She sits down and proceeds to do so.*]

Daisy. Harry is very anxious that you should like me.
Harry. George and I have known one another since we were kids. His people and mine live quite close to one another at home.
Daisy. But I'm not blaming you. I'm only wondering how I shall ingratiate myself with him.
Harry. He looks rather severe, but he isn't really. I think you've only got to be your natural charming self.
Daisy. Have you told him about the house?
Harry. No. [*To George.*] You know the temple the Harrisons used to have. We've taken that.
George. Oh, it's a ripping place. But won't you find it rather a nuisance to have those old monks on the top of you all the time?
Harry. Oh, I don't think so. Our part is quite separate, you know, and the Harrisons made it very comfortable.

75

[Harold Knox *comes in. He has changed into tennis things.*]

Knox. I say, Harry ... [*He sees* Daisy.] Oh, I beg your pardon.
Harry. Mr. Knox—Mrs. Rathbone.

[Knox *gives her a curt nod, but she holds out her hand affably. He takes it.*]

Daisy. How do you do.
Knox. I'm sorry to disturb you, Harry, but old Ku Faung Min is downstairs and wants to see you.
Harry. Tell him to go to blazes. The office is closed.
Knox. He's going to Hankow to-night and he says he must see you before he goes. He's got some big order to give.
Harry. Oh, curse him. I know what he is. He'll keep me talking for half an hour. D'you mind if I leave you?
Daisy. Of course not. It'll give me a chance of making Mr. Conway's acquaintance.
Harry. I'll get rid of him as quickly as I can.

[*He goes out accompanied by Knox.*

Knox. [*As he goes.*] Good-bye.

[George *looks at* Daisy *for a moment. She smiles at him. There is a silence.*]

George. Why didn't you warn me that it was you I was going to meet?
Daisy. I didn't know what you'd say about me to Harry if you knew.
George. It was rather a risk, wasn't it? Supposing I'd blurted out the truth.
Daisy. I trusted to your diplomatic training. Besides, I'd prepared for it. I told him I thought I'd met you.
George. Harry and I have been pals all our lives. I brought him out to China and I got him his job. When he had cholera he would have died if I hadn't pulled him through.
Daisy. I know. And in return he worships the ground you tread on. I've never known one man think so much of another as he does of you.
George. All that's rot, of course. Sometimes I don't know how I'm going to live up to the good opinion Harry has of me. But when

76

you've done so much for a pal as I have for him it gives you an awful sense of responsibility towards him.

Daisy. What do you mean by that?

[*A short pause.*]

George. I'm not going to let you marry him.

Daisy. He's so much in love with me that he doesn't know what to do with himself.

George. I know he is. But if you were in love with him you wouldn't be so sure of it.

Daisy. [*With a sudden change of tone.*] Why not? I was sure of your love. And God knows I was in love with you.

[George *makes a gesture of dismay. He is taken aback for a moment, but he quickly recovers.*]

George. You don't know what sort of a man Harry is. He's not like the fellows you've been used to. He's never knocked around as most of us do. He's always been as straight as a die.

Daisy. I know.

George. Have mercy on him. Even if there were nothing else against you he's not the sort of chap for you to marry. He's awfully English.

Daisy. If he doesn't mind marrying a Eurasian I really don't see what business it is of yours.

George. But you know very well that that isn't the only thing against you.

Daisy. I haven't an idea what you mean.

George. Haven't you? You forget the war. When we heard there was a very pretty young woman, apparently with plenty of money, living at the Hong Kong Hotel on very familiar terms with a lot of naval fellows, it became our business to make enquiries. I think I know everything there is against you.

Daisy. Have you any right to make use of information you've acquired officially?

George. Don't be a fool, Daisy.

Daisy. [*Passionately.*] Tell him then. You'll break his heart. You'll make him utterly wretched. But he'll marry me all the same. When a man's as much in love as he is he'll forgive everything.

George. I think it's horrible. If you loved him you couldn't marry him. It's heartless.

Daisy. [*Violently.*] How dare you say that? You. You. You know what I am. Yes, it's all true. I don't know what you know but it

77

can't be worse than the truth. And whose fault is it? Yours. If I'm rotten it's you who made me rotten.

George. I? No. You've got no right to say that. It's cruel. It's infamous.

Daisy. I've touched you at last, have I? Because you know it's true. Don't you remember when I first came to Chung-king? I was seventeen. My father had sent me to England to school when I was seven. I never saw him for ten years. And at last he wrote and said I was to come back to China. You came and met me on the boat and told me my father had had a stroke and was dead. You took me to the Presbyterian mission.

George. That was my job. I was awfully sorry for you.

Daisy. And then in a day or two you came and told me that my father hadn't left anything and what there was went to his relations in England.

George. Naturally he didn't expect to die.

Daisy. [*Passionately.*] If he was going to leave me like that why didn't he let me stay with my Chinese mother? Why did he bring me up like a lady? Oh, it was cruel.

George. Yes. It was unpardonable.

Daisy. I was so lonely and so frightened. You seemed to be sorry for me. You were the only person who was really kind to me. You were practically the first man I'd known. I loved you. I thought you loved me. Oh, say that you loved me then, George.

George. You know I did.

Daisy. I was very innocent in those days. I thought that when two people loved one another they married. I wasn't a Eurasian then, George. I was like any other English girl. If you'd married me I shouldn't be what I am now. But they took you away from me. You never even said good-bye to me. You wrote and told me you'd been transferred to Canton.

George. I couldn't say good-bye to you, Daisy. They said that if I married you I'd have to leave the service. I was absolutely penniless. They dinned it into my ears that if a white man marries a Eurasian he's done for. I wouldn't listen to them, but in my heart I knew it was true.

Daisy. I don't blame you. You wanted to get on, and you have, haven't you? You're Assistant Chinese Secretary already and Harry says you'll be Minister before you've done. It seems rather hard that I should have had to pay the price.

George. Daisy, you'll never know what anguish I suffered. I can't expect you to care. It's very natural if you hate me. I was ambitious. I didn't want to be a failure. I knew that it was madness to marry you. I had to kill my love. I couldn't. It was stronger than I was. At last I couldn't help myself. I made up my mind to chuck everything and take the consequences. I was just starting for Chungking when I heard you were living in Shanghai with a rich Chinaman.

[Daisy *gives a little moan. There is a silence.*]

Daisy. They hated me at the mission. They found fault with me from morning till night. They blamed me because you wanted to marry me and they treated me as if I was a designing cat. When you went away they heaved a sigh of relief. Then they started to convert me. They thought I'd better become a school teacher. They hated me because I was seventeen. They hated me because I was pretty. Oh, the brutes. They killed all the religion I'd got. There was only one person who seemed to care if I was alive or dead. That was my mother. Oh, I was so ashamed the first time I saw her. At school in England I'd told them so often that she was a Chinese princess that I almost believed it myself. My mother was a dirty little ugly Chinawoman. I'd forgotten all my Chinese and I had to talk to her in English. She asked me if I'd like to go to Shanghai with her. I was ready to do anything in the world to get away from the mission and I thought in Shanghai I shouldn't be so far away from you. They didn't want me to go, but they couldn't keep me against my will. When we got to Shanghai she sold me to Lee Tai Cheng for two thousand dollars.

George. How terrible.

Daisy. I've never had a chance. Oh, George, isn't it possible for a woman to turn over a new leaf? You say that Harry's good and kind. Don't you see what that means to me? Because he'll think me good I shall be good. After all, he couldn't have fallen in love with me if I'd been entirely worthless. I hate the life I've led. I want to go straight. I swear I'll make him a good wife. Oh, George, if you ever loved me have pity on me. If Harry doesn't marry me I'm done.

George. How can a marriage be happy that's founded on a tissue of lies?

Daisy. I've never told Harry a single lie.

George. You told him you hadn't been happily married.

Daisy. That wasn't a lie.

George. You haven't been married at all.

Daisy. [*With a roguish look.*] Well then, I haven't been happily married, have I?

George. Who was this fellow Rathbone?

Daisy. He was an American in business at Singapore. I met

him in Shanghai. I hated Lee. Rathbone asked me to go to Singapore with him and I went. I lived with him for four years.

George. Then you went back to Lee Tai Cheng.

Daisy. Rathbone died. There was nothing else to do. My mother was always nagging me to go back to him. He's rich and she makes a good thing out of it.

George. I thought she was dead.

Daisy. No. I told Harry she was because I thought it would make it easier for him.

George. She isn't with you now, is she?

Daisy. No, she lives at Ichang. She doesn't bother me as long as I send her something every month.

George. Why did you tell Harry that you were twenty-two? It's ten years since you came to China and you were seventeen then.

Daisy. [*With a twinkle in her eye.*] Any woman of my age will tell you that seventeen and ten are twenty-two.

[George *does not smile. With frowning brow he walks up and down.*]

George. Oh, I wish to God I knew nothing about you. I can't bring myself to tell him and yet how can I let him marry you in absolute ignorance? Oh, Daisy, for your sake as well as for his I beseech you to tell him the whole truth and let him decide for himself.

Daisy. And break his heart? There's not a missionary who believes in God as he believes in me. If he loses his trust in me he loses everything. Tell him if you think you must, if you have no pity, if you have no regret for all the shame and misery you brought on me, you, you, you—but if you do, I swear, I swear to God that I shall kill myself. I won't go back to that hateful life.

[*He looks at her earnestly for a moment.*]

George. I don't know if I'm doing right or wrong. I shall tell him nothing.

[Daisy *gives a deep sigh of relief*, Harry *comes in.*]

Harry. I say, I'm awfully sorry to have been so long. I couldn't get the old blighter to go.

Daisy. [*With complete self-control.*] If I say you've been an age it'll look as though Mr. Conway had been boring me.

Harry. I hope you've made friends.

Daisy. [*To* George.] Have we?

George. I hope so. But now I think I must bolt. I have a long Chinese document to translate. [*Holding out his hand to* Daisy.] I hope you'll both be very happy.

Daisy. I think I'm going to like you.

George. Good-bye, Harry, old man.

Harry. I shall see you later on in the club, sha'n't I?

George. If I can get through my work.

[*He goes out.*]

Harry. What have you and George been talking about?

Daisy. We discussed the house. It'll be great fun buying the things for it.

Harry. I could have killed that old Chink for keeping me so long. I grudge every minute that I spend away from you.

Daisy. It's nice to be loved.

Harry. You do love me a little, don't you?

Daisy. A little more than a little, my lamb.

Harry. I wish I were more worth your while. You've made me feel so dissatisfied with myself. I'm such a rotter.

Daisy. You're not going to disagree with me already.

Harry. What about?

Daisy. About you. I think you're a perfect duck.

[*The* Amah *appears.*]

Harry. Hulloa, who's this?

Daisy. Oh, it's my amah.

Harry. I didn't recognize her for a moment.

Daisy. She doesn't approve of my being alone with strange gentlemen. She looks after me as if I was a child of ten.

Amah. Velly late, missy Daisy. Time you come along.

Harry. Oh, nonsense.

Daisy. She wants me to go and be fitted. She never lets me go out in Peking alone.

Harry. She's quite right.

Daisy. Amah, come and be introduced to the gentleman. He's going to be your master now.

Amah. [*Smiling, with little nods.*] Velly nice gentleman. You keep missy Daisy old amah—yes? Velly good amah—yes?

Daisy. She's been with me ever since I was a child.

Harry. Of course we'll keep her. She was with you when you were in Singapore?

81

Daisy. [*With a little sigh.*] Yes, I don't know what I should have done without her sometimes.

Harry. Oh, Daisy, I do want to make you forget all the unhappiness you have suffered.

[*He takes her in his arms and kisses her on the lips. The* Amah *chuckles to herself silently.*]

END OF SCENE II

SCENE III

Scene: *The Temple of Fidelity and Virtuous Inclination. The courtyard of the temple is shown. At the back is the sanctuary in which is seen the altar table; on this are two large vases in each of which are seven lotus flowers, gilt but discoloured by incense, and in the middle there is a sand-box in which are burning joss-sticks; behind is the image of Buddha. The sanctuary can be closed by huge doors. These are now open. A flight of steps leads up to it.*

A service is finishing. The monks are seen on each side of the altar kneeling in two rows. They are clad in grey gowns and their heads are shaven. They sing the invocation to Buddha, repeating the same words over and over again in a monotonous chaunt. Daisy *stands outside the sanctuary door, on the steps, listlessly. The* Amah *is squatting by her side. Now the service ends; the monks form a procession and two by two, still singing, come down the steps and go out. A tiny acolyte blows out the oil lamps and with an effort shuts the temple doors.*

Daisy *comes down the steps and sits on one of the lower ones. She is dreadfully bored.*

Amah. What is the matter with my pletty one?

Daisy. What should be the matter?

Amah. [*With a snigger.*] Hi, hi. Old amah got velly good eyes in her head.

Daisy. [*As though talking to herself.*] I've got a husband who adores me and a nice house to live in. I've got a position and as much money as I want. I'm safe. I'm respectable. I ought to be happy.

Amah. I say, Harry no good, what for you wanchee marry? You say, I wanchee marry, I wanchee marry? Well, you married. What you want now?

Daisy. They say life is short. Good God, how long the days are.

Amah. You want pony—Harry give you pony. You want jade ring—Harry give you jade ring. You want sable coat—Harry give you sable coat. Why you not happy?

Daisy. I never said I wasn't happy.

Amah. Hi, hi.

Daisy. If you laugh like that I'll kill you.

Amah. You no kill old amah. You want old amah. I got something velly pletty for my little Daisy flower.

83

Daisy. Don't be an old fool. I'm not a child any more. [*Desperately.*] I'm growing older, older, older. And every day is just like every other day. I might as well be dead.

Amah. Look this pletty present old amah have got.

[*She takes a jade necklace out of her sleeve and puts it, smiling, into Daisy's hand.*]

Daisy. [*With sudden vivacity,*] Oh, what a lovely chain. It's beautiful jade. How much do they want for it?

Amah. It's a present for my little Daisy.

Daisy. For me? It must have cost five hundred dollars. Who is it from?

Amah. To-day is my little Daisy's wedding-day. She have married one year. Perhaps old amah want to give her little flower present.

Daisy. YOU! Have you ever given me anything but a beating?

Amah. Lee Tai Cheng pay me necklace and say you give to Daisy.

Daisy. You old hag. [*She flings the necklace away violently.*]

Amah. You silly. Worth plenty money. You no wanchee, I sell rich Amelican.

[*She is just going after the necklace, when* Daisy *catches her violently by the arm.*]

Daisy. How dare you? How dare you? I told you that you were never to let Lee Tai speak to you again.

Amah. You very angry, Daisy. You very angry before, but you go back to Lee Tai; he think perhaps you go back again.

Daisy. Tell him that I loathe the sight of him. Tell him that if I were starving I wouldn't take a penny from him. Tell him that if he dares to come round here I'll have him beaten till he screams.

Amah. Hi, hi.

Daisy. And you leave me alone, will you. Harry hates you. I've only got to say a word and he'll kick you out in five minutes.

Amah. What would my little Daisy do without old amah, hi, hi? What for you no talkee true? You think old amah no got eyes? [*With a cunning, arch look.*] I got something make you very glad.

[*She takes a note out of her sleeve.*]

Daisy. What's that?

Amah. I got letter.

Daisy. [*Snatching it from her.*] Give it me. How dare you hide it?

Amah. Have come when you long Harry. I think perhaps you no wanchee read when Harry there. [Daisy *tears it open.*] What he say?

Daisy. [*Reading.*] "I'm awfully sorry I can't dine with you on Thursday, but I'm engaged. I've just remembered it's your wedding-day and I'll look in for a minute. Ask Harry if he'd like to ride with me."

Amah. Is that all?

Daisy. "Yours ever. George Conway."

Amah. You love him very much, George Conway?

Daisy. [*Taking no notice of her, passionately.*] At last. I haven't seen him for ten days. Ten mortal days. Oh, I want him. I want him.

Amah. Why you no talkee old amah?

Daisy. [*Desperately.*] I can't help myself. Oh, I love him so. What shall I do? I can't live without him. If you don't want me to die make him love me.

Amah. You see, you want old amah.

Daisy. Oh, I'm so unhappy. I think I shall go mad.

Amah. Sh, sh. Perhaps he love you too.

Daisy. Never. He hates me. Why does he avoid me? He never comes here. At first he was always looking in. He used to come out and dine two or three days a week. What have I done to him? He only comes now because he does not want to offend Harry. Harry, Harry, what do I care for Harry?

Amah. Sh. Don't let him see. Give amah the letter.

[*She snatches it from* Daisy *and hides it in her dress as* Harry *comes in.* Daisy *pulls herself together.*]

Harry. I say, Daisy, I've just had the ponies saddled. Put on your habit and let's go for a ride.

Daisy. I've got a headache.

Harry. Oh, my poor child. Why don't you lie down?

Daisy. I thought I was better in the air. But there's no reason why you shouldn't ride.

Harry. Oh, no, I won't ride without you.

Daisy. Why on earth not? It'll do you good. You know when my head's bad I only want to be left alone. Your pony wants exercising.

Harry. The boy can do that.

85

Daisy. [*Trying to conceal her growing exasperation.*] Please do as I ask. I'd rather you went.

Harry. [*Laughing.*] Of course if you're so anxious to get rid of me....

Daisy. [*Smiling.*] I can't bear that you should be done out of your ride. If you won't go alone you'll just force me to come with you.

Harry. I'll go. Give me a kiss before I do. [*She puts up her lips to his.*] I'm almost ashamed of myself, I'm just as madly in love with you as the day we were married.

Daisy. You are a dear. Have a nice ride, and when you come back I shall be all right.

Harry. That's ripping. I shan't be very long.

[*He goes out. The lightness, the smile, with which she has spoken to Harry disappear as he goes, and she looks worried and anxious.*]

Daisy. Supposing they meet?

Amah. No can. Harry go out back way.

Daisy. Yes, I suppose he will. I wish he'd be quick. [*Violently.*] I must see George.

Amah. [*Picking up the necklace.*] Velly pletty necklace. You silly girl. Why you no take?

Daisy. Oh, damn, why can't you leave me alone? [*Listening.*] What on earth is Harry doing? I thought the pony was saddled.

Amah. [*Looking at the necklace.*] What shall I do with this?

Daisy. Throw it in the dust-bin.

Amah. Lee Tai no likee that very much.

Daisy. [*Hearing the sound of the pony, with a sigh of relief.*] He's gone. Now I'm safe. Where's my bag? [*She takes a little mirror out of it and looks at herself.*] I look perfectly hideous.

Amah. Don't be silly. You velly pletty girl.

Daisy. [*Her ears all alert.*] There's someone riding along.

Amah. That not pony. That Peking cart.

Daisy. You old fool, I tell you it's a pony. At last. Oh, my heart's beating so.... It's stopping at the gate. It's George. Oh, I love him. I love him. [*To the* Amah, *stamping her foot.*] What are you waiting for? I don't want you here now, and don't listen, d'you hear. Get out, get out.

Amah. All-light. My go away.

[*The* Amah *slinks away.* Daisy *stands waiting for* George, *holding her hands to her heart as though to stop the anguish of its beating.*

She makes a great effort at self-control as George *enters. He is in riding kit. He has a bunch of orchids in his hand.]*

George. Hulloa, what are you doing here?

Daisy. I was tired of sitting in the drawing-room.

George. I remembered it was your wedding-day. I've brought you a few flowers. [*She takes them with both hands.*]

Daisy. Thank you. That *is* kind of you.

George. [*Gravely.*] I hope you'll always be very happy. I hope you'll allow me to say how grateful I am that you've given Harry so much happiness.

Daisy. You're very solemn. One would almost think you'd prepared that pretty speech beforehand.

George. [*Trying to take it lightly.*] I'm sorry if it didn't sound natural. I can promise you it was sincere.

Daisy. Shall we sit down?

George. I think we ought to go for our ride while the light lasts. I'll come in and have a drink on the way back.

Daisy. Harry's out.

George. Is he? I sent you a note this morning. I said I couldn't dine on Thursday and I'd come and fetch Harry for a ride this afternoon.

Daisy. I didn't tell him.

George. No?

Daisy. I don't see you very often nowadays.

George. There's an awful lot of work to do just now. They lead me a dog's life at the legation.

Daisy. Even at night? At first you used to come and dine with us two or three nights a week.

George. I can't always be sponging on you. It's positively indecent.

Daisy. We don't know many people. It's not always very lively here. I should have thought if you didn't care to come for my sake you'd have come for Harry's.

George. I come whenever you ask me.

Daisy. You haven't been here for a month.

George. It just happens that the last two or three times you've asked me to dine I've been engaged.

Daisy. [*Her voice breaking.*] You promised that we'd be friends. What have I done to turn you against me?

George. [*His armour pierced by the emotion in her voice.*] Oh, Daisy, don't speak like that.

Daisy. I've tried to do everything I could to please you. If there's anything I do that you don't like, won't you tell me? I promise you I won't do it.

George. Oh, my dear child, you make me feel such an awful beast.

Daisy. Is it the past that you can't forget?

George. Good heavens, no, what do I care about the past?

Daisy. I have so few friends. I'm so awfully fond of you, George.

George. I don't think I've given you much cause to be that.

Daisy. There must be some reason why you won't ever come near me. Why won't you tell me?

George. Oh, it's absurd, you're making a mountain out of a molehill.

Daisy. You used to be so jolly, and we used to laugh together. I looked forward so much to your coming here. What has changed you?

George. Nothing has changed me.

Daisy. [*With a passion of despair.*] Oh, I might as well batter my head against a brick wall. How can you be so unkind to me?

George. For God's sake ... [*He stops.*] Heaven knows, I don't want to be unkind to you.

Daisy. Then why do you treat me as an outcast? Oh, it's cruel, cruel.

[George *is excessively distressed. He walks up and down, frowning. He cannot bear to look at* Daisy *and he speaks with hesitation.*]

George. You'll think me an awful rotter, Daisy, but you can't think me more of a rotter than I think myself. I don't know how to say it. It seems such an awful thing to say. I'm so ashamed of myself. I don't suppose two men have ever been greater pals than Harry and I. He's married to you and he's awfully in love with you. And I think you're in love with him. I was only twenty-three when I—first knew you. It's an awful long time ago, isn't it? There are some wounds that never quite heal, you know. Oh, my God, don't you understand? [*His embarrassment, the distraction of his tone, and the way the halting words fall unwillingly from his lips have betrayed the truth to* Daisy. *She does not speak, she does not stir, she looks at him with great shining eyes. She hardly dares to breathe.*] If ever you wanted revenge on me you've got it now. You must see that it's better that I shouldn't come here too often. Forgive me—Goodby.

[*He hurries away with averted face.* Daisy *stands motionless, erect; she is almost transfigured. She draws a long breath.*]

88

Daisy. Oh, God! He loves me.

[*She takes the orchids he has brought her and crushes them to her heart. The* Amah *appears.*]

Amah. You wantchee buy Manchu dress, Daisy?
Daisy. Go away.
Amah. Velly cheap. You look see. No likee, no buy.
Daisy. [*Impatiently.*] I'm sick of curio-dealers.
Amah. Velly pletty Manchu dresses.

[*She draws aside a little and allows a man with a large bundle wrapped up in a blue cotton cloth to come in. He is a Chinese. He is dressed in a long black robe and a round black cap. It is* Lee Tai Cheng. *He is big and rather stout. From his smooth and yellow face his black eyes gleam craftily. He lays his bundle on the ground and unties it, showing a pile of gorgeous Manchu dresses. Daisy has taken no notice of him. Suddenly she sees that a man, with his back turned to her, is there.*]

Daisy. [*To the* Amah.] I told you I wouldn't see the man. Send him away at once.
Lee Tai. [*Turning round, with a sly smile.*] You look see. No likee, no buy.
Daisy. [*With a start of surprise and dismay.*] Lee!
Lee Tai. [*Coming forward coolly.*] Good afternoon, Daisy.
Daisy. [*Recovering herself.*] It's lucky for you I'm in a good temper or I'd have you thrown out by the boys. What have you brought this junk for?
Lee Tai. A curio-dealer can come and go and no one wonders.
Amah. Lee Tai velly clever man.
Daisy. Give me that chain. [*The* Amah *takes it out of her sleeve and gives it to her.* Daisy *flings it contemptuously at* Lee Tai's *feet.*] Take it. Pack up your things and go. If you ever dare to show your face here again, I'll tell my husband.
Lee Tai. [*With a chuckle.*] What will you tell him? Don't you be a silly girl, Daisy.
Daisy. What do you want?
Lee Tai. [*Coolly.*] You.
Daisy. Don't you know that I loathe you? You disgust me.
Lee Tai. What do I care? Perhaps if you loved me I shouldn't want you. Your hatred is like a sharp and bitter sauce that tickles my appetite.
Daisy. You beast.

Lee Tai. I like the horror that makes your body tremble when I hold you in my arms. And sometimes the horror turns on a sudden into a wild tempest of passion.

Daisy. You liar.

Lee Tai. Leave this stupid white man. What is he to you?

Daisy. He is my husband.

Lee Tai. It is a year to-day since you were married. What has marriage done for you? You thought when you married a white man you'd become a white woman. Do you think they can look at you and forget? How many white women do you know? How many friends have you got? You're a prisoner. I'll take you to Singapore or Calcutta. Don't you want to amuse yourself? Do you want to go to Europe? I'll take you to Paris. I'll give you more money to spend in a week than your husband earns in a year.

Daisy. I'm very comfortable in Peking, thank you.

Lee Tai. [*Snapping his fingers.*] You don't care that for your husband. He loves you. You despise him. Don't you wish with all your heart that you hadn't married him?

Amah. He very silly white man. He no likee Daisy's old amah. Perhaps one day he b'long sick. Daisy cry velly much if he die?

Daisy. [*Impatiently.*] Don't be such a fool.

Amah. Perhaps one day he drink whisky soda. Oh, velly ill, velly ill. What's the matter with me? No sabe. No can stand. Doctor no sabe. Then die. Hi, hi.

Daisy. You silly old woman. Harry's not a Chinaman and he wouldn't call in a Chinese doctor.

Lee Tai. [*With a smile.*] China is a very old and a highly civilized country, Daisy. When anyone is in your way, it's not very difficult to get rid of him.

Daisy. [*Scornfully.*] And do you think I'd let poor Harry be murdered so that I might be free to listen to your generous proposals? You must think I'm a fool if you expect me to risk my neck for that.

Lee Tai. You don't take *any* risk, Daisy. You know nothing.

Amah. Lee Tai velly clever man, Daisy.

Daisy. I thought so once. Lee Tai, you're a damned fool. Get out.

Lee Tai. Freedom is a very good thing, Daisy.

Daisy. What should I do with it?

Lee Tai. Wouldn't you like to be free now? [*She looks at him sharply. She wonders if it can possibly be that he suspects her passion for George Conway. He meets her glance steadily.*] One day Sen Shi Ming was sitting with his wife looking at a Tang bronze that he had just bought when he heard someone in the street crying for help. Sen Shi was a very brave man and he snatched up a revolver and ran out. Sen Shi forgot that he had cheated his brother out of a house in Hatamen Street or he would have been more prudent. Sen Shi was found by the watchman an hour later with a dagger in his heart. Who killed cock-robin?

Amah. Hi, hi. Sen Shi velly silly man.

Lee Tai. His brother knew that. They had grown up together. If I heard cries for help outside my house late in the night, I should ask myself who had a grudge against me, and I should make sure the door was bolted. But white men are very brave. White men don't know the Chinese customs. Would you be very sorry if an accident happened to your excellent husband?

Daisy. I wonder what you take me for?

Lee Tai. Why do you pretend to me, Daisy? Do you think I don't know you?

Daisy. The door is a little on the left of you, Lee Tai. Would you give yourself the trouble of walking through it?

Lee Tai. [*With a smile.*] I go, but I come back. Perhaps you'll change your mind.

[*He ties up his bundle and is about to go.* Harry *enters.*]

Daisy. Oh, Harry, you're back very soon!

Harry. Yes, the pony went lame. Fortunately I hadn't gone far before I noticed it. Who's this?

Daisy. It's a curio-dealer. He has nothing I want. I was just sending him away.

[Lee Tai *takes up his bundle and goes out.*]

Harry. [*Noticing the orchids.*] Someone been sending you flowers?

Daisy. George.

Harry. Rather nice of him. [*To the* Amah.] Run along, amah, I want to talk to missy.

Amah. All light.

Harry. And don't let me catch you listening round the corner.

Amah. My no listen. What for I listen?

Harry. Run along—chop-chop.

Amah. Can do. [*She goes out.*]

Harry. [*With a laugh.*] I couldn't give you a greater proof of my affection than consenting to have that old woman around all the time.

Daisy. I don't know why you dislike her. She's devoted to me.

Harry. That's the only reason I put up with her. She gives me the creeps. I have the impression that she watches every movement I make.

Daisy. Oh, what nonsense!

Harry. And I've caught her eavesdropping.

Daisy. Was it amah that you wanted to talk to me about?

Harry. No, I've got something to tell you. How would you like to leave Peking?

Daisy. [*With a start, suddenly off her guard.*] Not at all.

Harry. I'm afraid it's awfully dull for you here, darling.

Daisy. I don't find it so.

Harry. You're so dear and sweet. Are you sure you don't say that on my account?

Daisy. I'm very fond of Peking.

Harry. We've been married a year now. I don't want to hurt your feelings, darling, but it's no good beating about the bush, and I think it's better to be frank.

Daisy. Surely you can say anything you like to me without hesitation.

Harry. Things have been a little awkward in a way. The women I used to know before we married left cards on you—

Daisy. Having taken the precaution to discover that I should be out.

Harry. And you returned those cards and that was the end of it. I asked George what he thought about my taking you to the club to play tennis and he said he thought we'd better not risk it. The result is that you don't know a soul.

Daisy. Have I complained?

Harry. You've been most awfully decent about it, but I hate to think of your spending day after day entirely by yourself. It can't be good for you to be so much alone.

Daisy. I might have known Mrs. Chuan. She's a white woman.

Harry. Oh, my dear, she was—heaven knows what she was! She's married to a Chinaman. It's horrible. She's outside the pale.

Daisy. And there's Bertha Raymond. She's very nice, even though she is a Eurasian.

Harry. I'm sure she's very nice, but we couldn't very well have the Raymonds here and refuse to go to them. Her brother is one of the clerks in my office. I don't want to seem an awful snob....

Daisy. You needn't hesitate to say anything about the Eurasians. You can't hate and despise them more than I do.

Harry. I don't hate and despise them. I think that's odious. But sometimes they're not very tactful. I don't know that I much want one of my clerks to come and slap me on the back in the office and call me old chap.

Daisy. Of course not.

Harry. The fact is we've been trying to do an impossible thing. It's no good kicking against the pricks. What with the legations and one thing and another Peking's hopeless. We'd far better clear out.

Daisy. But if I don't mind why should you?

Harry. Well, it's not very nice for me either. It's for my sake just as much as for yours that I'd be glad to go elsewhere. Of course everybody at the club knows I'm married. Some of them ignore it altogether. I don't mind that so much. Some of them ask after you with an exaggerated cordiality which is rather offensive. And every now and then some fool begins to slang the Eurasians and everybody kicks him under the table. Then he remembers about me and goes scarlet. By God, it's hell.

Daisy. [Sulkily.] I don't want to leave Peking. I'm very happy here.

Harry. Well, darling, I've applied for a transfer.

Daisy. [With sudden indignation.] Without saying a word to me?

Harry. I thought you'd be glad. I didn't want to say anything till it was settled.

Daisy. Do you think I am a child to have everything arranged for me without a word? [Trying to control herself.] After all, you'd never see George. Surely you don't want to lose sight of your only real friend.

Harry. I've talked it over with George and he thinks it's the best thing to do.

Daisy. Did he advise you to go?

Harry. Strongly.

Daisy. [Violently.] I won't do it. I won't leave Peking.

Harry. Why should his advice make the difference?

Daisy. Why? [She is confused for a moment, but quickly recovers herself.] I won't let George Conway—or anybody else—decide where I'm to go.

Harry. Don't be unreasonable, darling.

Daisy. I won't go. I tell you I won't go.

Harry. Well, I'm afraid you must now. It's all settled. The transfer is decided.

Daisy. [Bursting into tears.] Oh, Harry, don't take me away from here. I can't bear it. I want to stay here.

Harry. Oh, darling, how can you be so silly! You'll have a much better time at one of the outports. You see, there are so few white people there that they can't afford to put on frills. They'll be jolly glad to know us both. We shall lead a normal life and be like everybody else.

Daisy. [*Sulkily.*] Where do you want to go?

Harry. I've been put in charge of our place at Chung-king.

Daisy. [*Starting up with a cry.*] Chung-king! Of course you'd choose Chung-king.

Harry. Why, what's wrong with it? Do you know it?

Daisy. No—oh, what am I talking about? I'm all confused. Yes, I was there once when I was a girl. It's a hateful place.

Harry. Oh, nonsense! The consul's got a charming wife, and there are quite a nice lot of people there.

Daisy. [*Distracted.*] Oh, what shall I do? I'm so unhappy. If you cared for me at all you wouldn't treat me so cruelly. You're ashamed of me. You want to hide me. Why should I bury myself in a hole two thousand miles up the river? I won't go! I won't go! I won't go! [*She bursts into a storm of hysterical weeping.*]

Harry. [*Trying to take her in his arms.*] Oh, Daisy, for God's sake don't cry. You know I'm not ashamed of you. I love you more than ever. I love you with all my heart.

Daisy. [*Drawing away from him.*] Don't touch me. Leave me alone. I hate you.

Harry. Don't say that, Daisy. It hurts me frightfully.

Daisy. Oh, go away, go away!

Harry. [*Seeking to reason with her.*] I can't leave you like this.

Daisy. Go, go, go, go, go! I don't want to see you! Oh, God, what shall I do?

[*She flings herself doom on the steps, weeping hysterically. Harry, much distressed, looks at her in perplexity. The Amah comes in.*]

Amah. You make missy cly. You velly bad man.

Harry. What the devil do you want?

Amah. [*Going up to Daisy and stroking her head.*] What thing he talkee my poor little flower? Maskee. He belong velly bad man.

Harry. Shut up, you old ... I won't have you talk like that. I've put up with a good deal from you, but if you try to make mischief between Daisy and me, by God, I'll throw you out into the street with my own hands.

Amah. What thing you do my Daisy? Don't cly, Daisy.

Harry. Darling, don't be unreasonable.

Daisy. Go away, don't come near me. I hate you.

Harry. How *can* you say anything so unkind?

Daisy. Send him away. [*She begins to sob again more violently.*]

94

Amah. You go away. You no can see she no wanchee you. You come back bimeby. My sabe talk to little flower.

[*Harry hesitates for a moment. He is harassed by the scene. Then he makes up his mind the best thing is to leave Daisy with the Amah. He goes out. Daisy raises her head cautiously.*]

Daisy. Has he gone?

Amah. Yes. He go drink whisky soda.

Daisy. Do you know what he wants?

Amah. What for he tell me no listen? So fashion I sabe he say something I wanchee hear. He wanchee you leave Peking.

Daisy. I won't go.

Amah. Harry velly silly man. He alla same pig. You pull thisa way, he pull thata way. If Harry say you go from Peking—you go.

Daisy. Never, never, never!

Amah. You go away from Peking you never see George anymore.

Daisy. I should die. Oh, I want him! I want him to love me. I want him to hurt me. I want.... [*In her passion she has dug her hands hard into the* Amah.]

Amah. [*Pushing away* Daisy's *hands.*] Oh!

Daisy. He loves me. That's the only thing that matters. All the rest....

Amah. Harry wanchee you go Chung-king. Missionary ladies like see you again, Daisy. Perhaps they ask you how you like living along Lee Tai Cheng. Perhaps somebody tell Harry.

Daisy. The fool. Of all the places in China he must hit upon Chung-king.

Amah. You know Harry. If he say go Chung-king, he go. You cly, he velly solly, he all same go.

Daisy. Oh, I know his obstinacy. When he's once made up his mind—[*Contemptuously.*]—he prides himself on his firmness. Oh, what shall I do?

Amah. I think more better something happen to Harry.

Daisy. No, no, no!

Amah. What you flightened for? You no do anything. I tell Lee Tai more better something happen to Harry. I say you not velly sorry if Harry die.

Daisy. [*Putting her hands over her ears.*] Be quiet! I won't listen to you.

Amah. [*Roughly tearing her hands away.*] Don't you be such a big fool, Daisy. You go to Chung-king and Harry know everything. Maybe he kill you.

95

Daisy. What do I care?

Amah. You go to Chung-king, you never see George no more. George, he love my little Daisy. When Harry gone—George, he come say....

Daisy. Oh, don't tempt me, it's horrible!

Amah. He put his arms round you and you feel such a little small thing, you hear his heart beat quick, quick against your heart. And he throw back your head and he kiss you. And you think you die, little flower.

Daisy. Oh, I love him, I love him!

Amah. Hi, hi.

Daisy. [*Thinking of the scene with George.*] He would hardly look at me and his hands were trembling. He was as white as a sheet.

Amah. [*Persuasively.*] I tell you, Daisy. You no say yes, you no say no. I ask Buddha.

Daisy. [*Frightened.*] What for?

Amah. If Buddha say yes, I talk with Lee Tai; if Buddha say no, I do nothing. Then you go to Chung-king and you never see George any more.

[*The* Amah *goes up the temple steps and flings open the great doors.* Daisy *watches her with an agony of horror, expectation, and dread. The* Amah *lights some joss-sticks on the altar, and strikes a deep-toned gong.* Harry *comes in, followed by* Lee Tai *with his bundle.*]

Harry. [*Anxious to make his peace.*] Daisy, I found this fellow hanging about in the courtyard. I thought I'd like to buy you a Manchu dress that he's got.

Daisy. [*After a moment's reflection, with a change of tone.*] That's very nice of you, Harry.

Harry. It's a real beauty. You'll look stunning in it.

Lee Tai. [*Showing the dress, speaking in Pidgin English.*] Firs class dless. He belong Manchu plincess. Manchus no got money. No got money, no can chow. Manchus sell velly cheap. You takee, Missy.

[Daisy *and* Lee Tai *exchange glances.* Daisy *is grave and tragic, whereas* Lee Tai *has an ironical glint in his eyes. Meanwhile the* Amah *has been bowing before the altar. She goes down on her knees and knocks her head on the ground.*]

Harry. What in God's Name is amah doing?

Daisy. She's asking Buddha a question.

Harry. What question?

Daisy. [*With a shadow of a smile.*] How should I know?

Harry. What's the idea?

Daisy. Haven't you ever seen the Chinese do it? You see those pieces of wood she's holding in her hands. She's holding them out to the Buddha so that he may see them and she's telling him that he must answer the question. [*Meanwhile the* Amah, *muttering in a low tone, is seen doing what* Daisy *describes.*] The Buddha smells the incense of the burning joss-sticks, and he's pleased and he listens to what she says.

Harry. [*Smiling.*] Don't be so absurd, Daisy. One might almost think you believed all this nonsense. Why, you're quite pale.

Daisy. Then she gets up. The pieces of wood are flat on one side and round on the other. She'll lift them above her head and she'll drop them in front of the Buddha. If they fall with the round side uppermost it means yes. [Daisy *has been growing more and more excited as the ceremony proceeds. Now the* Amah *steps back a little and she raises her arms.* Daisy *gives a shriek and starts to run forward.*] No! no! Stop!

Harry. [*Instinctively seizing her arms.*] Daisy!

[*At the same moment the* Amah *has let the pieces of wood fall. She looks at them for an instant and then turns round.*]

Amah. Buddha talkee, can do.

Daisy. [*To* Harry.] Why did you stop me?

Harry. Daisy, how can you be so superstitious? What is the result?

Daisy. Amah asked Buddha a question and the answer is yes. [*She puts her hand to her heart for an instant, then looking at* Harry *she smiles.*] I'm sorry I was silly and unreasonable just now, Harry.

END OF SCENE III

SCENE IV

The sitting-room in the Andersons' *apartments. At the back are two double doors. The lower part of them is solid, but above they are cut in an intricate trellis. The ceiling is raftered, painted red and decorated with dim, gold dragons; the walls are whitewashed. On them hang Chinese pictures on rolls. Between the doors is a little image of the domestic god, and under it a tiny oil lamp is burning. The furniture is partly Chinese and partly European. There is an English writing-table, but the occasional tables, richly carved, are Chinese. There is a Chinese pallet-bed, covered with bamboo matting, and there is an English Chesterfield. There are a couple of Philippine rattan chairs and one or two of Cantonese blackwood. On the floor is a Chinese carpet. A Ming tile here and there gives a vivid note of colour. It is a summer night and the doors are wide open. Through them you see one of the courtyards of the temple.*

The Amah *is seated in one of the blackwood chairs by the side of a table. She has her water-pipe. She puts a pinch of tobacco in and then going to the lamp under the image lights a taper. She seats herself again and lights her pipe. She smokes quietly.*

Daisy *comes in. She wears an evening dress somewhat too splendid for dinner with only her husband and a friend.*

Amah. B. A. T. fellow, when he go?

Daisy. You know his name. Why don't you call him by it? I think he's going almost at once.

Amah. What for he go so soon?

Daisy. That's his business, isn't it? As a matter of fact his sister is arriving from England, and he has to go to meet her.

Amah. More better he go soon.

Daisy. Why do you smoke your pipe here? You know Harry doesn't like it.

Amah. Harry one big fool, I think. When you go to Chung-king?

Daisy. Harry hasn't said a word about it since.

Amah. You got key that desk?

Daisy. No. Harry keeps all his private papers there.

[*The* Amah *goes up to the desk and tries one of the drawers. It is locked and she cannot open it.*]

Amah. What Harry do now?

Daisy. He and Mr. Knox are drinking their port.

[*The* Amah *takes out a skeleton key out of her pocket and inserts it in the lock. She turns the key.*]

Amah. Velly bad lock. I think him made in Germany. Hi, hi. [*She opens the drawer and takes out a revolver. She hands it to* Daisy.] Lee Tai say, you take out cartridges.

Daisy. What do you mean? [*She suddenly guesses the truth and gives a cry.*] Oh!

Amah. [*Hurriedly putting her hand over* Daisy's *mouth.*] Sh, you no make noise. [*Holding out the revolver.*] Lee Tai say, more better you do it.

Daisy. Take it away. No, no, I won't, I won't.

Amah. Sh, sh. I do it. I sabe.

[*She takes the cartridges out of the revolver and hides them about her.* Daisy *looks at her with horror.*]

Daisy. It's not for to-night?

Amah. I no sabe.

Daisy. I won't have it. Do you hear? Oh, I shall go mad!

Amah. Then Harry shut you up. Hi, hi. All same Chung-king.

[*She puts the revolver back into the drawer and shuts it just as* Harry *and* Harold Knox *come in. They wear dinner jackets.*]

Knox. Hulloa, there's the little ray of sunshine. I missed your bonny face before dinner.

Amah. You velly funny man.

Knox. No wonder I dote upon you, dearie. You're the only attractive woman I've ever been able to persuade that I was a humourist.

Harry. [*Catching sight of the* Amah's *water-pipe.*] I told you I wouldn't have your disgusting pipe in here, amah.

Amah. Belong velly nice pipe.

Harry. I swore I'd throw the damned thing out myself if I found it lying about.

Amah. [*Snatching it away.*] You no touch my pipe. You velly bad man. Velly bad temper. You no Christian.

Harry. A fat lot you know about Christianity.

Amah. I know plentything about Christianity. My father velly poor man. He say, you go and be Christian. I go Catholic mission

99

and they baptize me. English Church missionary, he come along and say, Catholic mission no good, you go to hell, I baptize you. All right I say, you baptize me. By and by Baptist missionary come along and say, English Church mission no good, you go to hell, I baptize you. All right, I say, you baptize me. By and by Presbyterian missionary come along and say, Baptist mission no good, you go to hell, I baptize you. All right, I say, you baptize me. [*To* Knox.] You know Seventh Day Adventists?

Knox. I've heard of them.

Amah. By and by Seventh Day Adventist he come along and say, Presbyterian mission no good.

Knox. You go to hell.

Amah. How fashion you sabe what he said?

Knox. I guessed it.

Amah. You go to hell, he say. I baptize you. I been baptized one, two, three, four, five times. I velly Christian woman.

Harry. [*Smiling.*] I apologize.

Amah. They all say to poor Chinese, love one another. I no think missionaries love one another velly much. Hi, hi.

Knox. [*Taking out his watch.*] D'you mind if I look at the time? I don't want to get to the station late.

Harry. Of course not. I say, won't you have a cigar? [*He goes to his desk.*] I have to keep them locked up. I think the boys find them very much to their taste. [*He puts the key into the lock.*] Hulloa, the drawer's open. I could have sworn I locked it. [*He takes out a box of cigars and hands it to* Knox.]

Knox. [*Helping himself.*] Thanks very much.

Daisy. You know, you mustn't let me keep you if you want to be off.

Knox. I've got two or three minutes.

Harry. Oh, Daisy, before Harold goes I wish you'd show him that Manchu dress I bought you.

Daisy. I'll go and fetch it. [*To the* Amah.] Is it hanging up in the cupboard?

Amah. No, I have puttee in paper. I velly careful woman.

[They both go out.]

Knox. I say, old man, I hope you don't think I'm an awful swine to rush off like this the moment I've swallowed my dinner.

Harry. Rather not. As a matter of fact it's not exactly inconvenient, because I'm expecting George. I want him to have a heart to heart talk with Daisy.

Knox. Oh.

100

Harry. She's grousing rather about going to Chung-king and I want him to tell her it's a very decent place. He was vice-consul up there once. He's dining at the Carmichael's, but he said he'd come along here as soon as he could get away.

Knox. Then it's all for the best in the best of all possible worlds.

[Daisy *comes in with the dress.*]

Daisy. Here it is.

Knox. By George, isn't it stunning? I must try to get one for my sister. She'd simply go off her head if she saw that.

Daisy. Harry spoils me, doesn't he?

Knox. Harry's a very lucky young fellow to have you to spoil.

Daisy. [*Smiling.*] Go away or you'll never arrive in time.

Knox. I'm off. Goodby and thanks very much. Dinner was top-hole.

Daisy. Goodby.

[*He goes out.* Harry *accompanies him into the courtyard and for a moment is lost to view. The gaiety on* Daisy's *face vanishes and a look of anxiety takes its place.*]

Daisy. [*Calling hurriedly.*] Amah, amah.

Amah. [*Coming in.*] What thing?

Daisy. What have you done? Have you...? [*She stops, unable to complete the agonised question.*]

Amah. What you talk about? I done nothing. I only have joke with you. Hi, hi.

Daisy. Will you swear that's true?

Amah. Never tell a lie. Velly good Christian.

[Daisy *looks at her searchingly. She does not know whether to believe or not.* Harry *returns.*]

Harry. I say, Daisy, I wish you'd put on the dress. I'd love to see how you look in it.

Daisy. [*With a smile.*] Shall I?

Harry. Amah will help you. It'll suit you right down to the ground.

Daisy. Wait a minute. Bring the dress along, amah.

Amah. All right.

[Daisy *goes out, followed by the* Amah *with the Manchu dress.*

Harry *goes to his desk and opens the drawer. He examines the lock and looks at the keyhole.]*

Harry. [*To himself.*] I wonder if that old devil's got a key.

[He shuts the drawer, but does not lock it. He strolls back to the middle of the room.]

Daisy. [*In the adjoining room.*] Are you getting impatient?
Harry. Not a bit.
Daisy. I'm just ready.
Harry. I'm holding my breath. [Daisy *comes in. She is in full Manchu dress. She is strangely changed. There is nothing European about her any more. She is mysterious and enigmatical.*] Daisy! [*She gives him a little smile but does not answer. She stands quite still for him to look at her.*] By George, how Chinese you look!
Daisy. Don't you like it?
Harry. I don't know. You've just knocked me off my feet. Like it? You're wonderful. In my wildest dreams I never saw you like that. You've brought all the East into the room with you. My head reels as though I were drunk.
Daisy. It's strange that I feel as if these things were made for me. They make me feel so different.
Harry. I thought that no one in the world was more normal than I. I'm ashamed of myself. You're almost a stranger to me and by God, I feel as though the marrow of my bones were melting. I hear the East a-calling. I have such a pain in my heart. Oh, my pretty, my precious, I love you.

[He falls down on his knees before her and clasps both his arms round her.]

Daisy. [*In a low voice, hardly her own.*] Why, Harry, what are you talking about?

[She caresses his hair with her long, delicate Chinese hand.]

Harry. I'm such a fool. My heart is full of wonderful thoughts and I can only say that—that I worship the very ground you walk on.
Daisy. Don't kneel, Harry; that isn't the way a woman wants to be loved.

[She raises him to his feet and as he rises he takes her in his arms.]

102

Harry. [*Passionately.*] I'd do anything in the world for you.

Daisy. You could make me so happy if you chose.

Harry. I do choose.

Daisy. Won't you give up this idea of leaving Peking?

Harry. But, my darling, it's for your happiness I'm doing it.

Daisy. Don't you think that everyone is the best judge of his own happiness?

Harry. Not always.

Daisy. [*Disengaging herself from his arms.*] Ah, that's the English way. You want to make people happy in your way and not in theirs. You'll never be satisfied till the Chinese wear Norfolk jackets and eat roast beef and plum pudding.

Harry. Oh, my dear, don't let's argue now.

Daisy. You say you'll give me everything in the world and you won't give me the one thing I want. What's the good of offering me the moon if I have a nail in my shoe and you won't take it out?

Harry. Well, you can smile, so it's not very serious, is it?

Daisy. [*Putting her arms round his neck.*] Oh, Harry, I'll love you so much if you'll only do what I ask. You don't know me yet. Oh, Harry!

Harry. My darling, I love you with all my heart and soul, but when I've once made up my mind nothing on earth is going to make me change it. We can only be happy and natural if we go. You must submit to my judgment.

Daisy. How *can* you be so obstinate?

Harry. My dear, look at yourself in the glass now.

[*She looks down on her Manchu dress. She understands what he means. She is a Chinese woman.*]

Daisy. [*With a change of tone.*] Amah, bring me a tea-gown.

[*She begins to undo the long Manchu coat. The* Amah *comes in with a tea-gown.*]

Harry. [*Dryly.*] It's very convenient that you should always be within earshot when you're wanted, amah.

Amah. I velly good amah. Velly Christian woman.

[Daisy *slips off the Manchu clothes and is helped by the* Amah *into the tea-gown. She wraps it round her. She is once more a white woman.*]

Daisy. [*Pointing to the Manchu dress.*] Take those things away. [*To* Harry.] Would you like to have a game of chess?

Harry. Very much. I'll get the men.

[Daisy *goes to the gramophone and turns on a Chinese tune. It is strange and exotic. Its monotony exacerbates the nerves. Harry gets the chessboard and sets up the pieces. They sit down opposite one another. The* Amah *has disappeared with the discarded dress.*]

Harry. Will you take white?
Daisy. If you like. [*She moves a piece.*]
Harry. I hate your queen opening. It always flummoxes me. I don't know where you learned to play so well. I never have a chance against you.
Daisy. I was taught by a Chinaman. It's a game they take to naturally.

[*They make two or three moves without a word. Suddenly, breaking across the silence, stridently, there is a shriek outside in the street.* Daisy *gives a little gasp.*]

Harry. Hulloa, what's that?
Daisy. Oh, it's nothing. It's only some Chinese quarrelling.

[*Two or three shouts are heard and then an agonised cry of "Help, help."* Harry *springs to his feet.*]

Harry. By God, that's English.

[*He is just going to rush out when* Daisy *seizes his arm.*]

Daisy. What are you going to do? No, no, don't leave me, Harry.

[*She clings to him. He pushes her away violently.*]

Harry. Shut up. Don't be a fool.

[*He runs to the drawer of his desk. The cry is repeated: "For God's sake, help, help, oh!"*]

Harry. My God, they're killing someone. It can't be ... [*He remembers that George is coming that evening.*]
Daisy. [*Throwing herself on him.*] No, Harry, don't go, don't go, I won't let you.
Harry. Get out of my way.

[*He pushes her violently aside and runs out.* Daisy *sinks to the floor and buries her face in her hands.*]

Daisy. Oh, my God!

[*The* Amah *has been waiting just outside one of the doors, in the courtyard, and now she slips in.*]

Amah. Harry velly blave man. He hear white man being murdered. He run and help. Hi, hi.
Daisy. Oh, I can't. Harry, Harry.

[*She springs to her feet and runs towards the courtyard, with some instinctive idea of going to her husband's help.* The Amah *stops her.*]

Amah. What side you go?
Daisy. I can't stand here and let Harry be murdered.
Amah. You stop here.
Daisy. Let me go. For God's sake let me go. Wu, Wu.

[*The* Amah *puts her hand over* Daisy's *mouth.*]

Amah. You be quiet. You wanchee go prison?
Daisy. [*Snatching away her hand.*] I'll give you anything in the world if you'll only let me go.
Amah. You silly little fool, Daisy.

[Daisy *struggles to release herself, but she is helpless in the* Amah's *grasp.*]

Daisy. [*In an agony.*] It'll be too late.
Amah. Too late now. You no can help him.

[*She releases* Daisy. Daisy *staggers forward and covers her face with her hands.*]

Daisy. Oh, what have I done?
Amah. [*With a snigger.*] You no done nothing, you know nothing.
Daisy. [*Violently.*] Curse you! It's you, you, you!
Amah. I velly wicked woman. Curse me. Do me no harm.
Daisy. I told you I wouldn't have anything done to Harry.
Amah. You say no with your lips but in your belly you say yes.

105

Daisy. No, no, no!

Amah. You just big damned fool, Daisy. You no love Harry. Him not velly rich. Not velly big man. No good. You velly glad you finish with him.

Daisy. But not that way. He never did me any harm. He was always good to me and kind to me.

Amah. That velly good way. Velly safe way.

Daisy. You devil! I hate the sight of you.

Amah. What for you hate me? I do what you want. Your father velly clever man. He say: no break eggs, no can eat omelette.

Daisy. I wish I'd never been born.

Amah. [Impatiently.] What for you tell me lies? You want Harry dead. Well, I kill him for you. [With a sudden gust of anger.] You no curse me or I beat you. You velly bad girl.

Daisy. [Giving way.] Oh, I feel so awfully faint!

Amah. [Tenderly, as though Daisy were still a child.] You sit down. You take smelly salts. [She helps Daisy into a chair and holds smelling salts to her nostrils.] You feel better in a minute. Amah love her little Daisy flower. Harry him die and Daisy velly sorry. She cry and cry and cry. George velly sorry for Daisy. By and by Daisy no cry any more. She say, more better Harry dead. Good old amah, she do everything for little Daisy.

[Daisy has been looking at her with terrified eyes.]

Daisy. What a brute I am! I'd give anything in the world to have Harry back, and yet in the bottom of my heart there's a feeling—if I were free there'd be nothing to stand between George and me.

Amah. I think George he marry you maybe.

Daisy. Oh, not now! It'll bring me bad joss.

Amah. You no wanchee fear, my little flower. You sit still or you feel bad again.

Daisy. [Jumping up.] How can I sit still? The suspense is awful. Oh, my God, what's happened?

Amah. [With a cunning smile.] I tell you what's happened. Harry run outside and he see two, three men makee fighting. They a little way off. One man cry, "Help, help!" Harry give shout and run. He fall down and him not get up again.

Daisy. He's as strong as a horse. With his bare hands he's a match for ten Chinamen.

Amah. Lee Tai velly clever man. He no take risks. I think all finish now.

Daisy. Then for God's sake let me go.

Amah. More better you stay here, Daisy. Perhaps you get into trouble if you go out. They ask you why you go out,—why you think something happen to your husband.

Daisy. I can't let him lie there.

Amah. He no lie velly long. By and by night watchman come here, and he say white man in the street—him dead. I think his throat cut.

Daisy. Oh, how horrible! Harry, Harry!

[*She buries her face in her hands.*]

Amah. I light joss-stick. Make everything come all right.

[*She goes over to the household image and lights a joss-stick in front of it. She bows before it and going on her knees knocks her head on the ground.*]

Daisy. How long is it going on? How long have I got to wait? Oh, what have I done? The silence is awful. [*There is a silence. Suddenly* Daisy *breaks out into a shriek.*] No, no, no! I won't have it. I can't bear it. Oh, God help me! [*In the distance of the next courtyard is heard the chanting of the monks at the evening service. The* Amah, *having finished her devotions, stands at the doorway looking out steadily.* Daisy *stares straight in front of her. Suddenly there is a loud booming of a gong.* Daisy *starts up.*] What's that?

Amah. Be quiet, Daisy. Be careful.

[*The door of the courtyard is flung open.* Harry *comes in, through the courtyard, into the room, pushing before him a coolie whom he holds by the wrists and by the scruff of the neck.*]

Daisy. Harry!

Harry. I've got one of the blighters. [*Shouting.*] Here, bring me a rope.

Daisy. What's happened?

Harry. Wait a minute. Thank God, I got there when I did. [*Wu brings a rope and* Harry *ties the man's wrists behind his back.*] Keep quiet, you devil, or I'll break your ruddy neck. [*He slips the rope through the great iron ring of one of the doors and ties it so that the man cannot get away.*] He'll be all right there for the present. I'll just go and telephone to the police station. Wu, you stand outside there. You watch him. Sabe?

Wu. I sabe.

107

[*As Harry goes out a crowd of people surge through the great open doorway of the courtyard. They are monks of the temple, attracted to the street by the quick rumour of accident, coolies, and the night watchman with his rattle. Some of them bear Chinese lanterns, some hurricane lamps. The crowd separates out as they approach the room and then it is seen that three men are bearing what seems to be the body of a man.*]

Daisy. What's that?

Amah. I think belong foreign man. [*The men bring in the body and lay it on the sofa. The head and part of the chest are covered with a piece of blue cotton. Daisy and the Amah look at it with dismay. They dare not approach. The Abbot drives the crowd out of the room and shuts the doors, only leaving that side of one open at which the prisoner is attached. The Amah turns on the god in the niche.*] You say can do. What for you make mistake?

[*She seizes a fan which is on the table under her hand and with angry violence hits the image on the face two or three times. Daisy has been staring at the body. She goes up to it softly and lifts the cloth slightly, she gives a start, and with a quick gesture snatches it away. She sees George Conway.*]

Daisy. George. [*She opens her mouth to shriek.*]

Amah. Sh, take care. Harry hear.

Daisy. What have you done?

Amah. I do nothing. Buddha, he makee mistake.

Daisy. You fiend!

Amah. How do I know, Daisy? I no can tell George coming here to-night. [*The words come gurgling out, for Daisy has sprung upon her and seized her by the throat.*] Oh, let me go.

Daisy. You fiend.

[*Harry comes in. He is astounded at what he sees.*]

Harry. Daisy, Daisy. What in God's name are you doing?

[*Restrained by his voice, Daisy releases her hold of the Amah, but violently, pushing her so that she falls to the ground. She lies there, putting her hand to her throat. Daisy turns to HARRY.*]

Daisy. It's George.

Harry. [*Going up to the sofa and putting his hand on George's heart.*] Confound it, I know it's George.

Daisy. Is he dead?

Harry. No, he's only had a bang on the head. He's stunned. I've sent for the doctor. Luckily he was dining at the Carmichaels' and I sent George's rickshaw to bring him along as quick as he could come.

Daisy. Supposing he's gone?

Harry. He won't have gone. They were going to play poker. By God, what's this? [*He takes away his hand and sees blood upon it.*] He's been wounded. He's bleeding.

[Daisy *goes up to the body and kneeling down, feels the pulse.*]

Daisy. Are you sure he's alive?

Harry. Yes, his heart's beating all right. I wish the doctor would make haste. I don't know what one ought to do.

Daisy. How do you know he's at the Carmichaels'?

Harry. George told me yesterday he was going to be there. George said he did not want to play poker and he'd come along here after dinner.

Daisy. [*Springing to her feet.*] Did you know George was coming?

Harry. Of course I did. When I heard someone shouting in English the first thing I thought of was George.

[Daisy *bursts into a scream of hysterical laughter. The* Amah *suddenly looks up and becomes attentive.*]

Harry. Daisy, what's the matter?

Amah. [*Sliding to her feet and going up to Daisy, trying to stop her.*] Maskee. She only laughy laughy. You no trouble.

Harry. Get some water or something.

Amah. [*Frightened.*] Now, my pletty, my pletty.

Daisy. [*Recovering herself, violently.*] Let me be.

Harry. By George, I believe he's coming to. Bring the water here.

[Daisy *takes the glass and leaning over the sofa, moistens* George's *lips. He slowly opens his eyes.*]

George. Funny stuff. What is it?

Harry. [*With a chuckle that is half a sob.*] Don't be a fool. Oh, George, you have given me a nasty turn.

George. There's something the matter with the water.

Daisy. [*Looking at it quickly.*] What?

George. Damn it all, there's no brandy in it.
Daisy. If you make a joke I shall cry.

[*He tries to move, but suddenly gives a groan.*]

George. Oh Lord. I've got such a pain in my side.
Harry. Keep quiet. The doctor will be here in a minute.
George. What is it?
Harry. I don't know. There's a lot of blood.
George. I hope I haven't made a mess on your nice new sofa.
Harry. Damn the sofa. It's lucky I heard you shout.
George. I never shouted.
Harry. Oh, nonsense, I heard you. I thought it was you at once.
George. I heard a cry for help too. I was just coming along. I nipped out of my rickshaw and sprinted like hell. I saw some fellows struggling. I think someone hit me on the head. I don't remember much.
Harry. Who did cry for help?
George. [*After a pause.*] Nobody.
Harry. But I heard it. Daisy heard it too. It sounded like someone being murdered. [*As George *gives a little chuckle.*] What's the joke?
George. Someone's got his knife into you, old man, and the silly ass stuck it into me instead.

[*The* Amah *pricks up her ears.*]

Daisy. I'm sure you oughtn't to talk so much.
George. It's a very old Chinese trick. They just got the wrong man, that's all.
Harry. By George, that explains why I tripped.
George. Did you trip? A piece of string across the street.
Harry. I wasn't expecting it. I went down like a ninepin. I was up again in a flash and just threw myself at the blighters. You should have seen 'em scatter. Luckily I got one of them.
George. Good. Where is he?
Harry. He's here. I've tied him up pretty tight.
George. Well, we shall find out who's at the bottom of this. The methods of the Chinese police may be uncivilized, but they are ... Oh, Lord, I do feel rotten.
Harry. Oh, George.

[Daisy *gives* Harry *the glass and he helps* George *to drink.*]
110

George. That's better.

Harry. We'd better get you to bed, old man.

George. All right.

Harry. Wu and I will carry you. Wu, come along here.

[*The boy approaches. The* Amah *realizes that for a moment the prisoner is to be left unguarded. There is a table knife on one of the occasional tables with which* Daisy *has been cutting a book. The* Amah's *hand closes over it.*]

George. Oh, no, that's all right. I can walk.

[*He gets up from the sofa.* Harry *gives him an arm. He staggers.*]

Harry. Wu, you fool. [Daisy *springs forward.*] No, let me take him, Daisy. You're not strong enough.

George. [*Gasping.*] Sorry to make such an ass of myself.

[Harry *and* Wu, *holding him one on each side, help him out of the room.*]

Daisy. Shall I come?

Harry. Oh, I'll call you if you're wanted.

[Daisy *sinks into a chair, shuddering, and covers her face with her hands. The* Amah *seizes her opportunity. She cuts the rope which binds the prisoner. As soon as he is free he steps out into the darkness. The* Amah *watches for a moment and then cries out.*]

Amah. Help, help!

[Daisy *springs up and* Harry *hurries in.*]

Harry. What's the matter?

Amah. Coolie. Him run away.

Harry. [*Looking at the place where he had been tied up.*] By God!

Amah. Missy feel velly ill. No can stand blood. Feel faint. I run fetch smelly salts and when I come back him gone. Him bad man.

[Harry *goes to the door and looks at the rope.*]

Harry. This rope's been cut.

111

Amah. Perhaps he have knife. Why you no look see before you tie him.

Harry. [*Looking at her sternly.*] How do you think he could get at a knife with his hands tied behind his back?

Amah. I no sabe. Maybe he have friend.

Harry. Didn't you hear anything, Daisy?

Daisy. No. I wasn't thinking about him. Oh, Harry, George isn't going to die, is he?

Harry. I hope not. I don't know what sort of a wound he's got. [*The* Amah, *thinking attention is withdrawn from her, is slipping away.*] No, you don't. You stop here.

Amah. What thing you wantchee?

Harry. You let that man go.

Amah. You velly silly man. What for I want let him go?

Harry. [*Pointing.*] What's that knife doing there? That's one of our knives.

Amah. Missy takey knife cutty book.

Harry. When I got into the street I wanted to fire my revolver to frighten them. There wasn't a cartridge in it. I always keep it loaded and locked up.

Amah. Revolver. I don't know him. I never have see revolver. Never. Never.

[*She makes a movement as though to go away. He seizes her wrist.*]

Harry. Stop.

Amah. My go chow. My belong velly hungly. You talk by and by.

Harry. If I hadn't come in just now, Daisy would have strangled you.

Amah. Daisy velly excited. She no sabe what she do. She never hurt old amah.

Harry. Why were you angry with her, Daisy?

Daisy. [*Frightened.*] I was beside myself. I don't know what I was doing.

Harry. [*With sudden suspicion.*] Are you trying to shield her?

Daisy. Of course not. Why on earth should I do that?

Harry. I suppose you look on it as a matter of no importance that she tried to kill me.

Daisy. Oh, Harry, how can you say anything so cruel? Why should she try and kill you?

Harry. I don't know. How do you expect me to guess what is at the back of a Chinese brain? She's hated me always.

Amah. You no love me velly much.

Harry. I've put up with her just because she was attached to you. I knew she was a liar and a thief. It was a trap and I escaped by a miracle. Only, George has got to suffer for it.

Daisy. Harry, you're nervous and excited.

Harry. What are you defending her for?

Daisy. I'm not defending her.

Harry. One would almost think she had some hold on you. I've never seen anyone let an amah behave as you let her behave.

Daisy. She's been with me since I was a child. She—she can't get it into her head that I'm grown up.

Harry. Well, I've had about enough of her. [*To the* Amah.] The police will be here in ten minutes and I shall give you in charge instead of the man you allowed to escape.

Amah. You give me policeman? I no have do wrong. What for you send me to prison?

Harry. I daresay you know what a Chinese prison is like better than I do. I don't think it'll be long before you find it worth while to tell the truth.

Daisy. [*With increasing nervousness.*] Oh, Harry, I don't think you ought to do anything before you've had time to think. After all, there's absolutely no proof.

Harry. [*Looking at her with perplexity.*] I don't understand. What is the mystery?

Daisy. There is no mystery. Only I can't bear the idea that my old amah should go to prison. She's been almost a mother to me for so many years.

[*There is a pause.* Harry *looks from* Daisy *to the* Amah.]

Harry. [*To the* Amah.] Then get out of here before the police come.

Amah. You talkee so quick. No can understand.

Harry. Yes, you can. Unless you're out of here in ten minutes I shall give you in charge ... Go while the going's good.

Amah. I think I go smoke pipe.

Harry. No, you don't, you get out quick or I'll throw you out myself.

Amah. You no throw me out and I no go to prison.

Harry. We'll soon see about that.

[*He seizes her roughly and is about to run her out into the courtyard.*]

113

Daisy. No, don't, Harry. She's my mother.

Harry. That!

[*He is aghast. He releases the* Amah. *He looks at her with horror.* Daisy *covers her face with her hands. The* Amah *gives a little snigger.*]

Amah. Yes, Daisy, my daughter. She no wanchee tell. I think she a little ashamed of her mother.

Harry. My God!

Amah. I velly pletty girl long time ago. Daisy's father, he call me his little lotus flower, he call me his little peach-blossom. By and by I no velly pletty girl any more and Daisy's father he call me you old witch. Witch, that's what he call me. Witch. He call me, you old hag. You velly bad man, I say to him. You no Christian. You go to hell, he say. All right, I say, you baptize me.

[Harry *turns away, with dismay, and repulsion. The* Amah *takes her pipe and lights it.*]

END OF SCENE IV

114

SCENE V

The courtyard in the Andersons' *part of the temple.*

At the back is the outer wall raised by two or three steps from the ground. From the top of the wall, projects a shallow roof of yellow tiles supported by wooden pillars painted red, shabby and rather weather-worn, and this roof is raised in the middle of the wall, where there is a huge wooden gateway. When this is opened the street is seen and on the other side of it a high, blank, white wall. The courtyard is paved with great flags. On each side of it are living rooms.

There is a long rattan chair; a round table and a couple of armchairs. George *is lying on the long chair, looking at an illustrated paper, and the* Amah *is seated on the ground, smoking her water-pipe.*

George. [*With a smile, putting down the paper.*] You're not as chatty as usual this afternoon, amah.

Amah. Suppose I got nothing to talk about I no talk.

George. You are an example to your sex, amah. Your price is above rubies.

Amah. No likee rubies velly much. No can sell velly much money.

George. In point of fact I wasn't thinking of giving you rubies, even reconstructed, but if I did I can't think you'd be so indelicate as to sell them.

Amah. I no think you velly funny man.

George. I was afraid you didn't. Would you think it funny if I sat on my hat?

Amah. Yes, I laugh then. Hi, hi.

George. The inscrutable heart of China expands to the self-same joke that convulses a duchess in London and a financier in New York.

Amah. You more better read the paper.

George. Where's Missy?

Amah. I think she in her room. You wanchee?

George. No.

Amah. I think she come by and by.

George. [*Looking at his watch.*] Mr. Anderson ought to be back from the office soon. [*There is a loud knocking at the door.*] Hulloa, who's that?

115

[*A* Servant *comes out of the house and going to the gateway withdraws the bolt.*]

Amah. I think doctor come see you, maybe.

George. Oh no, he's not coming to-day. He said he'd look in to-morrow before I started.

[*The* Amah *gets up and looks at the doorway of which now the* Servant *has opened one side.* Harold Knox *and his sister* Sylvia *are seen.*]

Knox. May we come in?

George. Good man. Of course.

[*They come towards* George. Sylvia *is a very pretty, simple, healthy, and attractive girl. She is dressed in a light summer frock. There is in her gait and manner something so spring-like and fresh that it is a pleasure to look at her.*]

Knox. I've brought my young sister along with me. [*As* George *rises to his feet.*] Don't get up. You needn't put on any frills for a chit like that.

George. Nonsense. I'm perfectly well. [*Shaking hands with* Sylvia.] How d'you do? My name is Conway.

Knox. I only omitted to inform her of that fact because she already knew it.

Sylvia. Strangely enough that happens to be true. But I wish you'd lie down again.

George. I'm sick of lying down. The doctor says I'm perfectly all right. I'm going home to-morrow.

Knox. [*Catching sight of the* Amah.] Hulloa, sweetheart, I didn't see you. Sylvia, I want you to know the only woman I've ever loved.

George. [*Smiling.*] This is Mrs. Anderson's amah.

Sylvia. [*With a little friendly nod.*] How do you do?

Amah. [*All in a breath.*] Velly well, thank you. How do you do? Velly well, thank you ... You Mr. Knox sister?

Sylvia. Yes.

Amah. You missionary lady?

Sylvia. No.

Amah. What for you come China then?

Sylvia. I came to see my brother.

Amah. How old are you?

Knox. Be truthful, Sylvia.

116

Sylvia. I'm twenty-two.

Amah. How many children you got?

Sylvia. I'm not married.

Amah. What for you no married if you twenty-two?

Sylvia. It does need an explanation, doesn't it? The truth is that nobody's asked me.

Knox. What a lie!

Amah. You come China catchee husband?

Sylvia. Certainly not.

Amah. You Christian?

Sylvia. Not a very good one, I'm afraid.

Amah. Who baptized you?

Sylvia. Well, you know, it's an awfully long time ago. I forget.

Knox. She's like me, amah, she's a Presbyterian.

Amah. You go to hell then. Only Seventh Day Adventists no go to hell.

Sylvia. It'll be rather crowded then, I'm afraid.

Amah. You only baptized once?

Sylvia. So far as I know.

Amah. I baptized one, two, three, four, five times. I velly Christian woman.

Knox. I say, old man, I don't want to dash your fond hopes, but in point of fact we didn't come here to see you.

George. Why not? Surely Miss Knox must want to see the principal sights of Peking.

Knox. The man is not a raving lunatic, Sylvia. His only delusion is that he's a humourist ... Sylvia thought she'd like to call on Mrs. Harry.

George. I'm sure Daisy will be very glad. Amah, go and tell Missy that there's a lady.

Amah. Can do.

[Exit.]

Knox. I say, have they caught any of those blighters who tried to kill you?

George. No, not a chance. They weren't after me, you know; they were after Harry.

Knox. Is there anyone who has a grudge against him?

George. I don't think so. He doesn't seem very keen on discussing the incident.

[Daisy *comes in.*]

117

Knox. Here she is. I've brought my sister to see you, Mrs. Harry.

Daisy. [*Shaking hands.*] How do you do?

Sylvia. What a wonderful place you live in!

Daisy. It's rather attractive, isn't it? You must see the temple before you go.

Sylvia. I'd love to.

Daisy. Do sit down. [*To* Knox.] What do you think of my patient?

Knox. I think he's a fraud. I never saw anyone look so robust.

Daisy. [*Delighted.*] He's made a wonderful recovery.

George. Thanks to you, Daisy. You can't think how she nursed me.

Knox. It was rather a narrow escape, wasn't it?

Daisy. For two days we thought he might die at any minute. It was—it was rather dreadful.

George. And do you know, all that time she never left me a minute. [*To* Daisy.] I don't know how I can ever thank you.

Daisy. Oh, well, Harry had his work. I didn't think he ought to be robbed of his night's rest for a worthless creature like you, and I hated the idea of a paid nurse looking after you.

Sylvia. You must have been worn out at the end of it.

Daisy. No, I'm as strong as a horse. And it was such a relief to me when the doctor said he was out of danger, I forgot I was tired.

Knox. I don't know why you bothered about him. There are such a lot of fellows who want his job and they all know they could do it much better than he can.

George. Everyone's been so extraordinarily good to me. I had no idea there was so much kindness in the world.

Daisy. [*To* Sylvia, *very pleasantly.*] Will you come and look at the temple now while they're bringing tea?

Sylvia. Yes, I'd like to very much.

Daisy. I think you'll enjoy your tea more if you feel you've done the sight.

Sylvia. It's all so new to me. Everything interests me. I've fallen passionately in love with Peking.

[*They wander off, talking gaily.*]

George. Harold, you're a very nice boy.

Knox. That's what the girls tell me. But I don't know why you should.

George. I think it was rather sporting of you to bring your sister to see Daisy.

Knox. I don't deserve any credit for that. She insisted on coming.

George. Oh?

Knox. She met Harry at the club and took rather a fancy to him. When I told her Daisy was a half-caste and people didn't bother much about her she got right up on her hind legs. I told her she'd only just come out to China and didn't know what she was talking about and then she gave me what she called a bit of her mind. I was obliged to remark that if that was a bit I didn't much care about knowing the rest.

George. It sounds as though you'd had a little tiff.

Knox. She said she had no patience with the airs people gave themselves in the East. A Eurasian was just as good as anybody else. And when I happened to say I was coming here to-day to see how you were she said she'd come too.

George. It's very kind of her. Daisy leads a dreadfully lonely life. It would mean so much to her if she knew one or two white women. If they take to one another, you won't try to crab it, will you? I fancy Daisy wants a friend rather badly.

Knox. I shouldn't like it very much, you know. Would you much care for your sister to be very pally with a half-caste?

George. Daisy is one in a thousand. You can't think what she's done for me during my illness. My mother couldn't have taken more care of me.

Knox. They're often very good-hearted. But as a matter of fact nothing I can say will have the least effect on Sylvia. Girls have changed a lot since the war. If she wants to do a thing and she thinks it right, she'll do it. And if I try to interfere she's quite capable of telling me to go to the devil.

George. She seems to be a young woman of some character.

Knox. Perhaps because she's had rather a rough time. The fellow she was engaged to was killed in the war and she was awfully cut up. She drove an ambulance for the last two years and then she went up to Girton. After that my father thought she'd better come out here for a bit.

George. She ought to like it.

Knox. If she doesn't put up people's backs too much. She can't stand anything like injustice or cruelty. If she thinks people are unkind to Daisy or sniffy about her, she'll stick to her like a leech. However, I daresay she'll get married.

George. [*Smiling.*] That'll learn her.

Knox. Why don't you marry her? It's about time you settled down.

George. [*With a chuckle.*] You fool.

Knox. Why? You're by way of being rather eligible, aren't you?

George. I don't know why you want to get rid of her. She seems a very nice sister.

Knox. Of course I love having her with me, but she does cramp my style a bit. And she ought to marry. She'd make you a first-rate wife.

George. Much too good for the likes of me.

Knox. Of course she's a bit independent, but one has to put up with that in girls nowadays. And she's as good as gold.

George. One can see that at a mile, my son.

Knox. I say, who was Rathbone, Daisy's first husband, do you know?

George. [*His face a blank.*] Harry told me he was an American. He said he was in business in the F. M. S.

Knox. That's what Harry told me. I met a fellow the other day who lives in Singapore who told me he'd never heard of Rathbone.

George. [*Chaffing him.*] Perhaps he didn't move in the exalted circles that a friend of yours would naturally move in.

Knox. I suppose there was a Mr. Rathbone?

[*There is a distant sound in the street of Chinese instruments being played.*]

George. Hulloa, there's the procession coming along.

Knox. What procession?

George. It's a Manchu wedding. The amah was talking about it this morning.

Knox. I must call Sylvia. She'd love to see it. Sylvia.

[Daisy *and* Sylvia *come out of the house just as he calls.*]

Sylvia. Don't shout, Harold.

Knox. Come along and have your education improved. A Manchu wedding is just going to pass by....

Sylvia. Oh, good, let's go out into the street!

Daisy. You can see it just as well from here. I'll have the doors opened. Boy, open the gate.

Knox. Yes, that's the ticket. We shall see it better from here.

[Wu *during the last few speeches has appeared with the tea, which he sets down on the table. On receiving* Daisy's *order he goes to the doorway and draws the bolt. He pulls back one heavy door while* Knox *pulls back the other. The empty street is seen. The music grows louder. Now the procession comes, gay, brilliant, and*

120

barbaric against the white wall of the street; first men on horseback, then Buddhist monks in gray, with their shaven heads; then the band, playing wild, discordant music; after them passes a long string of retainers in red, with strange shaped hats; then come retainers bearing in open palanquins great masses of cardboard fruits and all manner of foodstuffs, silver vessels and gold; these are followed by two or three youths on horseback, gorgeously dressed, and these again by the palanquin, carved and richly painted and gilt, of the bride. Then pass more priests and another band and finally a last string of retainers in red. When the last one has disappeared a beggar shows himself at the open doorway. He is excessively thin, and he has a bush of long, bristly hair; he is clothed in pale rags, torn and patched; his legs and feet are bare. He puts out a bony hand and breaks into a long, high-pitched whine.]

Knox. Oh, Lord, get out!

Daisy. Oh, no, please, Harold, give him a copper or two.

George. Daisy never lets a beggar go away without something.

Daisy. It's not because I'm charitable. I'm afraid they'll bring me bad luck.

Knox. [*Taking a coin from his pocket.*] Here you are, Clarence. Now buzz off.

[*The beggar takes his dole and saunters away.* Wu *closes the doors.*]

Sylvia. [*Enthusiastically.*] I *am* glad I saw that.

Daisy. You'll get very tired of that sort of thing before you've been here long. Now let's have tea.

Sylvia. Oh, I don't think we'll stay, thank you very much. We have another call to make.

Daisy. How tiresome of you. Harry ought to be back in a few minutes. He'll be disappointed not to have seen you.

Sylvia. I promised to go and see Mrs. Stopfort. Do you know her?

Daisy. I know who you mean.

Sylvia. I think people are being absolutely beastly to her. It simply makes my blood boil.

Daisy. Oh, how?

Sylvia. Well, you know that her husband's a drunken brute who's treated her abominably for years. At last she fell in love with a man and now her husband is going to divorce her. It's monstrous that he should be able to.

121

Daisy. Are the ladies of Peking giving her the cold shoulder?

Knox. The cold *shoulder* hardly describes it. The frozen silverside.

George. I think she's well rid of Reggie Stopfort at any price, but I'm sorry the other party is André Leroux.

Sylvia. Why? She introduced me to him. I thought he was a very nice fellow.

George. Well, you see, if he'd been English or American, he would have married her as a matter of course.

Sylvia. So I should hope.

Daisy. Because she was divorced on his account, you mean?

George. Yes. But the French haven't our feeling on that matter. I'm not quite sure if André will be willing to marry her.

Sylvia. Oh, that would be dreadful! Under those circumstances the man must marry the woman. He simply must.

George. Of course.

Knox. Come along, Sylvia. We won't discuss women's rights now.

Sylvia. [*Giving* Daisy *her hand very cordially.*] And if there's anything I hate it's people who say they're going and then don't go. Good-bye, Mrs. Anderson.

Daisy. It's been very nice to see you.

Sylvia. I do hope you'll come and see me soon. I'm so very much alone you'd be doing me a charity if you'd look me up. We might do the curio shops together.

Daisy. That would be great fun.

Sylvia. Good-bye, Mr. Conway. I'm glad to see you so well.

George. Thank you very much, good-bye.

[Knox *and* Sylvia *go out.* Daisy *has walked with them towards the doorway and now returns to* George.]

George. What a very nice girl, Daisy.

Daisy. She seems to make a specialty of speckled peaches. First me and then Mrs. Stopfort.

George. I was hoping you'd like her.

Daisy. It's hardly probable. She's everything that I'm not. She has everything that I haven't. No, I don't like her. But I'd give anything in the world to be her.

George. [*Smiling.*] I don't think you need envy her.

Daisy. Don't you think she's pretty?

George. Yes, very. But you're so much more than pretty. I expect you have more brains in your little finger than she has in her whole body.

Daisy. [*Gravely*.] She has something that I haven't got, George, and I'd give my soul to have.

George. [*Embarrassed*.] I don't know what you mean. [*Changing the conversation abruptly*.] Daisy, now that I'm going away....

Daisy. [*Interrupting*.] Are you really going to-morrow?

George. [*Breezily*.] I'm quite well. I'm ashamed to have stayed so long.

Daisy. I don't look forward very much to the long, empty days when you're no longer here.

George. [*Seriously*.] I must go, Daisy. I really must.

Daisy. [*After a moment's pause*.] What were you going to say to me? Don't thank me for anything I may have done. It's given me a happiness I never knew before.

George. Except for you I should have died. And when I think of the past I am ashamed.

Daisy. What does the past matter? The past is dead and gone.

George. And I'm ashamed when I think how patient you were when I was irritable, how kind and thoughtful. I hardly knew I wanted a thing before you gave it to me. Sometimes when I felt I couldn't breathe, the tenderness of your hand on my forehead—oh, it was like a dip in a highland stream on a summer day. I think I never knew that there was in you the most precious thing that anyone can have, goodness. Oh, Daisy, it makes me feel so humble.

Daisy. Goodness? [*With the shadow of a laugh*.] Oh, George.

George. It's because Harry is better and simpler than I am that he was able to see it in you. He felt it in you always and he was right.

[*The* Amah *comes in*.]

Daisy. [*Sharply*.] What d'you want?

[*The* Amah *crosses from one to the other and a thin smile crosses her eyes*.]

Amah. Master telephone, Daisy.

Daisy. Why didn't you take the message?

[*She is about to go into the house*.]

Amah. He have go now. He say very much hurry. I say no can findee you. I think you go out.

Daisy. Why did you say that?

Amah. I think more better, maybe.

George. [*Smiling.*] That's right, amah. Never tell the truth when a lie will do as well.

Daisy. Well, what was the message?

Amah. Master say he must to go Tientsin. Very important business. No come back to-night. Come back first train to-morrow.

Daisy. Very well. Tell the boy that we shall be only two to dinner.

Amah. I go talkee he.

[*Exit.*]

George. [*Urbanely.*] I say, I don't want to be an awful trouble to you. I think I'd better go back to my own place to-night.

Daisy. [*Looking at him.*] Why should you do that?

George. I was going to-morrow anyway.

Daisy. Do you think my reputation is such a sensitive flower?

George. [*Lightly.*] Of course not. But people aren't very charitable. It seems rather funny I should stay here when Harry's away.

Daisy. What do you suppose I care if people gossip?

George. I care for you.

Daisy. [*With a smile, almost archly.*] It's not very flattering to me that you should insist on going the moment Harry does. Do I bore you so much as all that?

George. [*With a chuckle.*] How can you talk such nonsense? I haven't wanted to get well too quickly. I've so enjoyed sitting quietly here while you read or sewed. I've got so much in the habit of seeing you about me that if I don't go at once I shall never be able to bring myself to go at all.

Daisy. Since that horrible accident I've been rather nervous at the thought of sleeping here by myself. I'm terrified at the thought of being left alone to-night.

George. Come in with me, then. The Knoxes will be delighted to put you up for the night.

Daisy. [*With a sudden change of manner.*] I don't want you to go, George. I want you to stay.

George. [*As serious as she is.*] Daisy, don't be too hard on me. You don't know. You don't know. [*With an effort he regains his self-control and returns to his easy, chaffing tone.*] Don't forget it's not only a wound in the lung that I've been suffering from. While you and the doctor between you have been patching that up, I've been busy sticking together the pieces of a broken heart. It's nicely set now, no one could tell that there'd ever been anything wrong with it, but I don't think it would be very wise to give it a sudden jolt or jerk.

Daisy. [*In a low quivering voice.*] Why do you say things like that? What is the good of making pretences?

George. [*Determined to keep the note of lightness.*] It was very silly of me to bother you with my little troubles. It was very hot. I was overworked and nervous at the time or I shouldn't have made so much of it. I'm sure that you'll be as pleased as I am to know that I'm making a very good recovery, thank you.

Daisy. [*As though asking a casual question.*] You don't care for me any more?

George. I have the greatest affection for you. I admire you and of course I'm grateful to you. But if I thought I was in love with you I was mistaken.

Daisy. Do you know why I wouldn't have a professional nurse and when you were unconscious for two days refused to leave you for a minute? Do you know why, afterwards, at night when you grew delirious I wouldn't let Harry watch you? I said it would interfere with his work. I dared not leave you for a single moment. And it was your secret and mine. I wouldn't let anybody in the world share it with me. Do you know what you said in your delirium?

George. [*Disturbed.*] I expect I talked an awful lot of rot. People always do, I believe.

Daisy. [*Passionately.*] You used to call me, "Daisy, Daisy," as though your heart was breaking. And when I leaned over you and said: "I'm here," you would take my face in your hands so that I could hardly believe you weren't conscious. And you said: "I love you."

George. Oh, God!

Daisy. And sometimes I didn't know how to calm you. You were frantic because you thought they were taking me away from you. "I can't bear it," you said, "I shall die." I had to put my hands over your mouth so that no one should hear.

George. I didn't know what I was saying. I wasn't myself. It was just the madness of the fever.

Daisy. And sometimes you were so exquisitely tender. Your voice was soft and caressing. And you called me by sweet names so that the tears ran down my cheeks. You thought you held me in your arms and you pressed me to your heart. You were happy then; you were so happy that I was afraid you'd die of it. I know what love is and you love me.

George. For God's sake, stop. Why do you torture me?

Daisy. And then you were madly jealous. You hated Harry. I think you could have killed him.

George. That's not true. That's infamous. Never. Never.

Daisy. Oh, you can say that with your lips! Sometimes you thought he put his arms round me and kissed me and you sobbed aloud. Oh, it was so painful. I forgot that you were unconscious and I took your hands and said: "He's not here. You and I are alone, alone, alone." And sometimes I think you understood. You fell back. And a look of peace came on your face as if you were in heaven and you said—do you know what you said? You said: "Beloved, beloved, beloved."

[*Her voice breaks and the tears course down her cheeks. George is shattered by what she has told him.*]

George. I suppose there are few of us that wouldn't turn away from ourselves in horror if the innermost thoughts of our heart, the thoughts we're only conscious of to hate, were laid bare. But that shameful thing that showed itself in me isn't me. I disown it....

Daisy. I thought you had more courage. I thought you had more sense. Do you call that you, a few conventional prejudices? The real you is the love that consumes you more hotly than ever the fever did. The only you is the you that loves me. The rest is only frills. It's a domino that you put on at a masked ball.

George. You don't know what you say. Frills? It's honour, and duty, and decency. It's everything that makes it possible for me to cling to the shadow of my self-respect.

Daisy. Oh, all that means nothing. You fool. You might as well try with your bare hands to stop the flow of the Yangtze.

George. If I perish I perish. Oh, of course I love you. All night I'm tortured with love and tortured with jealousy, but the day does come at last and then I can get hold of myself again. My love is some horrible thing gnawing at my heart-strings. I hate it and despise it. But I can fight it, fight it all the time. Oh, I've been here too long. I ought to have got back to work long ago. Work is my only chance. Daisy, I beseech you to let me go.

Daisy. How can I let you go? I love you.

George. [*Thunderstruck.*] You? [*Impatiently, with a shrug of the shoulders.*] Oh, you're talking nonsense.

Daisy. Why do you suppose I've said all these things? Do you think a woman cares twopence for a man's love when she doesn't love him?

George. Oh, it's impossible. You don't know what you're saying. I know how good and kind you are. You've been touched by my love. You mistake pity for love.

Daisy. I'm not good and I'm not kind. There's no room in my

soul for pity. In my soul there's only a raging hunger. If I know what you feel it's because I feel it too. I love you, I love you, I love you.

George. And Harry?

Daisy. What do I care about Harry? I hate him because he's stood between me and you.

George. He is your husband. He is my friend.

Daisy. He doesn't exist. I've loved you always from the first day I saw you. The others were nothing to me, Lee Tai and Harry and the rest. I've loved you always. I've never loved anyone but you. All these years I've kept the letters you wrote to me. I've read them till I know every word by heart. They're all blurred and smudged with the tears I've wept over them. They were all I had. Do you think I'm going to let you go now? All my pain, all my anguish, are nothing any more. I love you and you love me.

George. Oh, don't, don't!

Daisy. You can't leave me now. If you leave me I shall kill myself.

George. I must go away. I must never see you again. Whatever happens we must never meet.

Daisy. [*Exasperated and impatient.*] That's impossible. What will you say to Harry?

George. If need be I'll tell him the truth.

Daisy. What difference will that make? Will you love me any the less? Yes, tell him. Tell him that I love you and you only and that I belong to you and to you only.

George. Oh, Daisy, for God's sake try and control yourself. We must do our duty, we must, we must.

Daisy. I know no duty. I only know love. There's no room in my soul for anything else. You say that love is like a wild beast gnawing at your entrails. My love is a liberator. It's freed me from a hateful past. It's freed me from Harry. There's nothing in the world now but you and me and the love that joins us. I want you, I want you.

George. Don't, don't! Oh, this is madness! There's only one thing to be done. God, give me strength. Daisy, you know I love you. I love you with all my heart and soul. But it's good-bye. I'll never see you again. Never. Never. So help me God.

Daisy. How can you be so cruel? You're heartless. I've wanted you all these years. I've hungered for you. You don't know what my humiliation has been. Pity me because I loved you. If you leave me now I shall die. You open the doors of heaven to me and then you slam them in my face. Haven't you made me unhappy enough? You'd have done better to kill me ten years ago. You trampled me in the mud and then you left me. Oh, what shall I do? [*She sinks down*

127

to the ground, weeping as though her heart would break. George looks at her for a minute, his face distorted with agony; he clenches his hands in the violence of his effort to control himself. He takes his hat and walks slowly towards the gate. He withdraws the bolt that holds it. When Daisy hears the sound of this she starts to her feet and staggers towards him.] George. No, no. Not yet.

[She staggers and with a cry falls headlong. She has fainted.]

George. [Rushing towards her.] Daisy. Daisy. [He kneels down and takes her head in his hands. He is fearfully agitated.] Oh, my darling, what is it? Oh, my God! Daisy! Speak to me. [Calling.] Amah, amah! [Daisy slowly opens her eyes.] Oh, my beloved! I thought you were dead.
    Daisy. Lift me up.
    George. You can't stand.

[He raises her to her feet so that when she is erect she is in his arms. She puts her arms round his neck.]

    Daisy. Don't leave me.
    George. My precious. My beloved.

[She turns her face to him, offering her lips, and he bends his head and kisses her. She closes her eyes in ecstasy.]

    Daisy. Take me in. I feel so ill.
    George. I'll carry you.

[He lifts her up and carries her into the house. From the opposite side the Amah appears. She goes to the gateway and slips the bolt forward into position. Then she comes to the tea-table, sits down and takes a scone.]

    Amah. Hi, hi.

[She bites the scone and chews placidly. On her face is a smirk of irony.]

END OF SCENE V

SCENE VI

A small room in a Chinese house in Peking.

The walls are whitewashed, but the whitewash is not a little stained. Three or four scrolls hang on them, written over in large characters with inscriptions. On the floor is matting. The only furniture consists of a table, with a couple of chairs, a wooden pallet covered with matting, with cushions at one end of it, and a Korean chest heavily ornamented with brass. At the back are two windows, elaborately latticed and covered with rice paper, and a lightly carved door.

Daisy is seated in one of the chairs. She has taken her pocket mirror out of her bag and is looking at herself. She is gay and happy. The Amah comes in. She carries a long-necked vase in which are a couple of carnations.

Amah. I bring you flowers make room look pletty.

Daisy. Oh, you nice old thing! Put them on the table.

Amah. You look at yourself in looking-glass?

Daisy. I'm looking young. It suits me to be happy.

Amah. You very pletty girl. I very pletty girl long time ago. You look alla same me some day.

Daisy. [*Amused.*] Heaven forbid.

Amah. You velly good temper to-day, Daisy. You glad because George come.

Daisy. I didn't see him yesterday.

Amah. He keep you waiting.

Daisy. The wretch. He always keeps me waiting. But what do I care as long as he comes? We shall have three hours. Perhaps he'll dine here. If he says he can, give him what he likes to eat. No one can make such delicious things as you can if you want to.

Amah. You try flatter me.

Daisy. I don't. You know very well you're the best cook in China.

Amah. [*Tickled.*] Oh, Daisy! I know you more better than you think.

Daisy. You're a wicked old woman. [*She gives her a kiss on both cheeks.*] What are they making such a row about next door?

Amah. Coolie, he got killed this morning. He have two small children. Their mother, she die long time ago.

Daisy. How dreadful! Poor little things.

129

Amah. You like see them. They here.

[*She goes to the door and beckons. A little, old, shabby Chinaman comes in with two tiny children, a boy and a girl, one holding on to each hand. They are very solemn and shy and silent.*]

Daisy. Oh, what lambs!

Amah. They no got money. This old man he say he take them and he bring them up. But he only coolie. He no got much money himself.

Daisy. Is he related to them?

Amah. No, him just velly good man. He no can do velly much. He just do what he can. The neighbours, they help little.

Daisy. But I'll help too. Have you got any money on you?

Amah. I got two, three dollars.

Daisy. What's the good of that? Let him have this.

[*She has a chain of gold beads round her neck. She takes it off and puts it in the old man's hands.*]

Amah. That chain very ispensive, Daisy.

Daisy. What do I care? Let him sell it for what it'll fetch. It'll bring me luck. [*To the old man.*] You sabe?

[*He nods, smiling.*]

Amah. I think he understand all right.

Daisy. [*Looking at the children.*] Aren't they sweet? And so solemn. [*To the* Amah.] You go chop-chop to the toy shop opposite and buy them some toys.

Amah. Can do.

[*She goes out.* Daisy *takes the children and sets them up on the table.*]

Daisy. [*Charmingly.*] Now you come and talk to me. Sit very still now or you'll fall off. [*To the little boy.*] I wonder how old you are. [*To the old man.*] Wu? Liu?

Old Man. Liu.

Daisy. [*To the little boy.*] Six years old. Good gracious, you're quite a man. If I had a little boy he'd be older than you now. If I had a little boy I'd dress him in such smart things. And I'd bath him myself. I wouldn't let any horrid old amah bath him. And I wouldn't stuff him up with sweets like the Chinese do; I'd give him one piece

130

of chocolate when he was a good boy. Gracious me, I've got some chocolates here. Wait there. Sit quite still. [*She goes over to the shelf on which is a bag of chocolates*.] There's one for you and one for you and (*to the old man*) one for you. And here's one for me.

[*The children and the Chinaman eat the chocolates solemnly. The Amah returns with a doll and a child's Peking cart.*]

Amah. Have catchee toys.

Daisy. Look what kind old amah has brought you. [*She lifts the children off the table and gives the doll to the little girl and the cart to the boy*.] Here's a beautiful doll for you and here's a real cart for you. [*She sits down on the floor*.] Look, the wheels go round and everything.

Amah. Have got more presents.

[*She takes out of her sleeve little bladders with mouthpiece attached so that they can be blown up.*]

Daisy. What on earth is this? Oh, I love them! We must all have one. [*She distributes them and they all blow them up. There it the sound of scratching at the door*.] Who's that, I wonder?

Amah. If you say come in, perhaps you see.

Daisy. Open the door, you old silly. [*She begins to blow up the balloon again. The* Amah *goes to the door and opens it.* Lee Tai *steps in*.] Lee Tai. Send these away. [*The* Amah *makes a sign to the old Chinaman, he gives each child a hand and with their presents they go out. The* Amah *slips out after them*.] I thought you were dead.

Lee Tai. I'm very much alive, thank you.

Daisy. Ah, well, we'll hope for the best.

Lee Tai. I trust you're not displeased to see me.

Daisy. [*Gaily*.] If you'd come yesterday I should certainly have smacked your face, but to-day I'm in such a good humour that even the sight of you is tolerable.

Lee Tai. You weren't here yesterday.

[*The* Amah *comes in carrying on a little wooden tray, two Chinese bowls and a tea-pot.*]

Daisy. My dear Mamma seems to think you've come to pay me a visit. You mustn't let me keep you too long.

Lee Tai. You are expecting someone? I know.

131

[*The* Amah *goes out.*]

Daisy. [*Chaffing him.*] I always said you had a brain.

Lee Tai. No better a one than yours, Daisy. It was a clever trick when you got me to try to put your husband out of the way so that you should be free for George Conway.

Daisy. It was nothing to do with me. I told you I'd have nothing to do with it. You made a hash of it. One can forgive the good for being stupid, but when rascals are fools there's no excuse.

Lee Tai. The best laid schemes of mice and men, as my favourite poet Robert Burns so elegantly puts it, gang aft agley.

Daisy. I don't care a damn about your favourite poet. What have you come here for to-day?

Lee Tai. As it turns out I do not see that there is any cause for regret that George Conway got the knife thrust that was intended for your husband. I wish it had gone a little deeper.

Daisy. [*Coolly.*] As it turns out you only did me a service. But still you haven't told me to what I owe the honour of your visit.

Lee Tai. Civility. I like to be on friendly terms with my tenants.

Daisy. [*Surprised.*] Your what?

Lee Tai. [*Urbanely.*] This happens to be my house. When I discovered that your honourable mother had taken the rooms in this courtyard so that you might have a place where George Conway and you could safely meet I thought I would buy the whole house.

Daisy. I hope it was a good investment.

Lee Tai. Otherwise perhaps I should have hesitated. It was clever of you to find so convenient a place. With a curio shop in front into which anyone can be seen going without remark and an ill-lit passage leading to this court, it is perfect.

Daisy. What is the idea?

Lee Tai. [*With a twinkle in his eyes.*] Are you a little frightened?

Daisy. Not a bit. What can you do? You can tell Harry. Tell him.

Lee Tai. [*Affably.*] George Conway would be ruined.

Daisy. [*With a shrug.*] He'd lose his job. Perhaps you would give him another. You're mixed up in so many concerns you could surely find use for a white man who speaks Chinese as well as George does.

Lee Tai. I find even your shamelessness attractive.

Daisy. I'm profoundly grateful for the compliment.

Lee Tai. But do not fear. I shall do nothing. I bought this house because I like you to know that always, always you are in my

132

hand. Where you go, I go. Where you are, I am. Sometimes you do not see me, but nevertheless I am close. I do nothing. I am content to wait.

Daisy. Your time is your own. I have no objection to your wasting it.

Lee Tai. One day, and I think that day is not very far distant, you will come to me. I was the first and I shall be the last. If you like I will marry you.

Daisy. [*With a smile.*] I thought you had two, if not three, wives already. I fancy that number four would have rather a thin time.

Lee Tai. My wife can be divorced. I am willing to marry you before the British Consul. We will go to Penang. I have a house there. You shall have motor cars.

Daisy. It's astonishing how easy it is to resist temptations that don't tempt you.

Lee Tai. Sneer. What do I care? I wait.... What have you to do with white men? You are not a white woman. What power has this blood of your father's when it is mingled with the tumultuous stream which you have inherited through your mother from innumerable generations? Our race is very pure and very strong. Strange nations have overrun us, but in a little while we have absorbed them so that no trace of a foreign people is left in us. China is like the Yangtze, which is fed by five hundred streams and yet remains unchanged, the river of golden sand, majestic, turbulent, indifferent, and everlasting. What power have you to swim against that mighty current? You can wear European clothes and eat European food, but in your heart you are a Chinawoman. Are your passions the weak and vacillating passions of the white man? There is in your heart a simplicity which the white man can never fathom and a deviousness which he can never understand. Your soul is like a rice patch cleared in the middle of the jungle. All around the jungle hovers, watchful and jealous, and it is only by ceaseless labour that you can prevent its inroads. One day your labour will be vain and the jungle will take back its own. China is closing in on you.

Daisy. My poor Lee Tai, you're talking perfect nonsense.

Lee Tai. You're restless and unhappy and dissatisfied because you're struggling against instincts which were implanted in your breast when the white man was a hungry, naked savage. One day you will surrender. You will cast off the white woman like an outworn garment. You will come back to China as a tired child comes back to his mother. And in the immemorial usages of our great race you will find peace.

[*There is a moment's silence.* Daisy *passes her hand over her forehead. Against her will she is strangely impressed by what* Lee Tai *has said. She gives a little shudder and recovers herself.*]

Daisy. George Conway loves me, and I— Oh!

Lee Tai. The white man's love lasts no longer than a summer day. It is a red, red rose. Now it flaunts its scented beauty proudly in the sun and to-morrow its petals, wrinkled and stinking, lie scattered on the ground.

[*There is a sound of a footstep in the courtyard outside.*]

Daisy. Here he is. Go quickly.

[George *opens the door and stops as he catches sight of* Lee Tai.]

George. Hulloa, who's this?

[Lee Tai *steps forward, smiling and obsequious.*]

Lee Tai. I am the owner of this house. The amah complained that the roof leaked and I came to see for myself.

George. [*Frowning.*] It's of no consequence. Please don't bother about it.

Lee Tai. I wish I needn't. The amah has a virulent and active tongue—I am afraid she will give me no peace till I have satisfied her outrageous demands.

George. You speak extraordinarily good English.

Lee Tai. I am a graduate of the University of Edinburgh.

Daisy. Robert Burns is his favourite poet.

Lee Tai. I spent a year at Oxford and another at Harvard. I can express myself in English not without fluency.

George. Let me compliment you on your good sense in retaining your national costume. I think it a pity that the returned students should insist on wearing ugly tweed suits and billycock hats.

Lee Tai. I spent eight years abroad. I brought back with me no more admiration for Western dress than for Western civilization.

George. That is very interesting.

Lee Tai. You are pleased to be sarcastic.

George. And you, I think, are somewhat supercilious. Believe me, the time has passed when the mandarins of your country, in their impenetrable self-conceit, could put up a barrier against the advance of civilization. If you have any love for China you must see that her only chance to take her rightful place in the world is to accept honestly and sincerely the teaching of the West.

Lee Tai. And if in our hearts we despise and detest what you have to teach us? For what reason are you so confident that you are so superior to us that it behooves us to sit humbly at your feet? Have you excelled us in arts or letters? Have our thinkers been less profound than yours? Has our civilization been less elaborate, less complicated, less refined than yours? Why, when you lived in caves and clothed yourselves with skins we were a cultured people. Do you know that we tried an experiment which is unique in the world?

George. [*Good-naturedly.*] What experiment is that?

Lee Tai. We sought to rule this great people not by force, but by wisdom. And for centuries we succeeded. Then why does the white man despise the yellow? Shall I tell you?

George. Do.

Lee Tai. [*With a smiling contempt.*] Because he has invented the machine-gun. That is your superiority. We are a defenceless horde and you can blow us into eternity. [*With a tinge of sadness.*] You have shattered the dream of our philosophers that the world could be governed by the power of law and order.... And now you are teaching our young men your secret. You have thrust your hideous inventions upon us. Fools. Do you not know that we have a genius for mechanics? Do you not know that there are in this country four hundred millions of the most practical and industrious people in the world? Do you think it will take us long to learn? And what will become of your superiority when the yellow man can make as good guns as the white and fire them as straight? You have appealed to the machine-gun and by the machine-gun shall you be judged.

[*There is a pause. Suddenly* George *gives* Lee Tai *a scrutinizing glance.*]

George. What is your name?

Lee Tai. [*With a thin, amused smile.*] Lee Tai Cheng.

George. [*With a frigid politeness.*] I'm sure you are very busy, Mr. Lee. I won't detain you any longer.

Lee Tai. [*Still smiling.*] I wish you a good day.

[*He bows slightly and shakes his own hands in the Chinese manner. He goes out. He leaves behind him an impression that is at once ironic and sinister.*]

George. What the devil is he doing here?

135

Daisy. [*Amused.*] He came to make me an offer of marriage. I pointed out to him that I was married already.

George. [*Not without irritation.*] How did he know you were here?

Daisy. He made it his business to find out.

George. Does he know that...?

Daisy. [*Coolly.*] You know China better than most Englishmen. You know that the white man can do nothing without the Chinese knowing it. But they won't tell other white men unless—unless it's to their advantage to do so.

George. You told me that this house belonged to the amah.

Daisy. [*Smiling.*] That was a slight exaggeration.

George. You put it very mildly.

Daisy. You said you wouldn't come to the temple. It meant finding some place where we could meet or never seeing you at all.

George. [*Sombrely.*] We began with deceit and with deceit we've continued.

Daisy. [*Tenderly.*] There's no deceit in my love, George. After all, our love is the only thing that matters.

George. [*With a certain awkwardness.*] I'm afraid I've kept you waiting. André Leroux came to see me just as I was leaving the Legation.

Daisy. [*Remembering.*] I know. Mrs. Stopfort's young man.

George. He said he knew Mrs. Stopfort's friends were rather anxious about her future and he wanted them to know that he was going to marry her as soon as she was free.

Daisy. Oh!

George. Of course it's the only decent thing to do, but I wasn't sure if he'd see it. He's a very good fellow. [*With a smile.*] He spent at least half an hour telling me how he adored Mrs. Stopfort.

Daisy. [*Good-humouredly.*] Oh, you know I'm not the sort of woman to grouse because you're a little late. I can always occupy myself by thinking how wonderful it will be to see you. And if I get bored with that I read your letters again.

George. I shouldn't have thought they were worth that.

Daisy. I think I have every word you have ever written to me—those old letters of ten years ago and the little notes you write to me now. Even though they're only two or three lines, saying you'll come here or can't come, they're precious to me.

George. But do you keep them here?

Daisy. Yes, they're safe here. They're locked up in that box. Only amah has the key of this room ... George.

George. Yes.

Daisy. Will you do something for me?

George. If I can.

Daisy. Will you dine here to-night? Amah will get us a lovely little dinner.

George. Oh, my dear, I can't! I've got an official dinner that I can't possibly get out of.

Daisy. Oh, how rotten!

George. But I thought Harry was coming back this morning. He's been gone a week already.

Daisy. I had a letter saying he had to go on to Kalgan. But don't say anything about it. He told me I was to keep it a secret.

George. He must hate having to be away so much as he's been lately. The death of that man Gregson has upset things rather.

Daisy. [*Smiling.*] I wish I could thank Gregson for the good turn he did *us* by dying at the psychological moment.

George. [*Dryly.*] I don't suppose that was his intention.

Daisy. Except for that Harry would have insisted on going to Chung-king. Now there's no possibility of that for at least a year.

George. I suppose not.

Daisy. We've got a year before us, George, a whole year. And in a year anything can happen.

George. [*Gravely.*] Do you never have any feeling that we've behaved rottenly to Harry?

Daisy. I? I've been happy for the first time in my life. At last I've known peace and rest. Oh, George, I'm so grateful for all you've given me! In these three months you've changed the whole world for me. I thought I couldn't love you more than I did. I think every day my love grows more consuming.

George. [*With a sigh.*] I've never known a single moment's happiness.

Daisy. That's not true. When I've held you in my arms I've looked into your eyes and I've seen.

George. Oh, I know. There've been moments of madness in which I forgot everything but that I loved you. I'm a low rotten cad. No one could despise me more than I despise myself. I've loved you so that there was room for nothing else in my soul. Waking and sleeping you've obsessed me.

Daisy. That's how I want you to love me.

George. And I've hated myself for loving you. I've hated you for making me love you. I've struggled with all my might and a hundred times I thought I'd conquered myself and then the touch of your hand, the softness of your lips—I was like a bird in a cage, I beat myself against the bars and all the time the door was open and I hadn't the will to fly out.

Daisy. [*Tenderly.*] Oh, darling, why do you make yourself unhappy when happiness lies in the hollow of your hand?

George. Have you never regretted anything?

Daisy. Never.

George. You're stronger than I am. I'm as weak as dishwater. It's funny that it should have taken me all these years to find it out. I was weak from the beginning. But I was weakest of all that day. I was distracted, I thought you were dying, I forgot everything except that I loved you.

Daisy. [*With passion.*] Oh, my sweetheart! Don't you remember how, late in the night, we went outside the temple and looked at the moonlight on the walls of the Forbidden City? You had no regrets then.

George. [*Going on with his own thoughts.*] And afterwards your tears, your happiness, the dread of giving you pain and the hot love that burnt me—I was in the toils then. I too knew a happiness that I had never known before. On one side was honesty and duty and everything that makes a man respect himself—and on the other was love. I thought you'd be going away in two or three weeks and that would be the end of it. Oh, it was no excuse—there are no excuses for me, I can never look Harry in the face again, but though my heart was breaking at the thought, I—I knew that in a few days I should see you for the last time.

Daisy. [*Scornfully.*] Do you think I'd have gone then?

George. And then came that sudden, unexpected, disastrous change in all Harry's plans. And this house and all the sordid horror of an intrigue. And then there was nothing to do but face the fact that I was a cur. I wouldn't wish my worst enemy the torture that I've undergone.

Daisy. [*Full of love and pity.*] Oh, my darling, you know I'd do anything in the world to give you happiness!

George. [*Sombrely looking away from her.*] Daisy, I think you can never give me happiness, but you can help me, not to make amends because that's impossible, but to ... [*Impulsively, looking at her now.*] Oh, Daisy, do you really love me?

Daisy. With all my heart. With all my soul.

George. Then help me. Let us finish.

Daisy. [*Quickly.*] What do you mean?

George. I don't want to seem a prig. I don't want to preach. Heaven knows, I've never pretended to be a saint. But what we've done is wrong. You must see that as plainly as I do.

Daisy. Is it wrong to love? How can I help it?

George. Daisy, I want to—cease doing wrong.

Daisy. You make me impatient. How can you be so weak?

George. I want you to believe that I love you. But I can't go on with this deceit. I'd sooner shoot myself.

Daisy. You couldn't say that if you loved me as I love you.

George. [*Brutally.*] I *don't* love you any more.

Daisy. [*With a scornful shrug.*] That's not true.

George. [*Clenching his teeth.*] I came here to-day to tell you that—well, that it's finished and done with. Oh, God, I don't want to make you unhappy! But you must see we can't go on. Everything that's decent in me revolts at the thought. I beseech you to forget me.

Daisy. As if I could.

George. I'm going away for a bit.

Daisy. [*Startled.*] You? Why?

George. I didn't trust myself, you see; I've lost my nerve, so I applied for short leave. I'm sailing for Vancouver on the *Empress*. I leave here the day after to-morrow.

Daisy. [*Suddenly distraught.*] You don't mean that you're going to leave me? I didn't pay any attention to what you said. I thought it was just a mood. George, George, say that you don't mean that?

George. It's the only thing to do, for your sake and Harry's and mine. [*Taking his courage in both hands.*] This is good-bye, Daisy.

Daisy. [*Seizing him by the shoulders.*] Let me look at your eyes. George, you're crazy. You can't go.

George. [*Drawing away.*] For God's sake, don't touch me. I wanted to break it to you gently. I don't know what's happened. Everything has gone wrong. I'm going, Daisy, and nothing in the world can move me. I implore you to bear it bravely. [*She looks at him with suffering, anxious eyes. She is stunned.*] I'm afraid you're going to be awfully unhappy for a little while. But I beseech you to have courage. Soon the pain won't be so great, and then you'll see I've done the only possible thing.

Daisy. [*Sullenly.*] How long are you going for?

George. Three or four months. [*A pause.*] I knew you'd be brave, Daisy. Do you know, I was afraid you'd cry most awfully. It tears my heart to see you cry.

Daisy. Do you think I'm a child? Do you think I can cry now?

George. It's good-bye, then, Daisy.

[*She does not answer. She hardly hears what he says. He hesitates an instant wretchedly, and then goes quickly out of the room. Daisy stands as if she were turned to stone. Her face is haggard. In a minute Lee Tai comes softly in. He stands at the door, looking at her, then gives a little cough. She turns round and sees him.*]

Daisy. [*Fiercely.*] What do you want?

Lee Tai. I was waiting till you were disengaged.

Daisy. Have you been listening?

Lee Tai. I have heard.

Daisy. I wish I could have seen you with your ear to the keyhole. You must have looked dignified.

[*She begins to laugh, angrily, hysterically, beside herself.*]

Lee Tai. Let me give you a cup of tea. It's quite warm still.

Daisy. I should have thought you were rather old and fat to stoop so much.

Lee Tai. Fortunately the windows are only covered with rice paper, so I was saved that inconvenience.

[*He hands her a cup of tea. She takes it and flings it at him. The tea is splashed over his black robe.*]

Daisy. Get out of here or I'll kill you.

[*He wipes his dress with a large silk pocket handkerchief.*]

Lee Tai. You forget sometimes the manners that were taught you at that elegant school for young ladies in England.

Daisy. I suppose you've come to crow over me. Well, crow.

Lee Tai. I told you that I thought I should not have to wait very long.

Daisy. [*Scornfully.*] You fool. Do you think it's finished?

Lee Tai. Did I not tell you that the white man's love was weak and vacillating?

Daisy. He's going away for four months. Do you think that frightens me? He's loved me for ten years. I've loved him for ten years. Do you think he can forget me in four months? He'll come back.

Lee Tai. Not to you.

Daisy. Yes, yes, yes. And when he comes it'll be for good. He'll hunger for me as he hungered before. He'll forget his scruples, his remorse, his stupid duties, because he'll only remember me.

Lee Tai. [*Very quietly.*] He's going to be married to Miss Sylvia Knox.

[Daisy *springs at him and seizes him by the throat.*]

Daisy. That's a lie. That's a lie. Take it back. You pig.

140

[*He takes her hands and drags them away from his throat. He holds her fast.*]

Lee Tai. Ask your mother. She knows. The Chinese all know.

Daisy. [*Calling.*] Amah, amah. It's a lie. How dare you?

Lee Tai. He told you he was going to an official dinner, but he didn't tell you that as soon as he could get away he was going to play bridge at the Knoxes'. Pity you don't play. They might have asked you too.

[*The* Amah *comes in.*]

Amah. You call me, Daisy?

Daisy. [*Snatching her hands away.*] Let me go, you fool. [*To the* Amah.] He says George Conway is engaged to Harold Knox's sister. It's not true.

Amah. I no sabe. George's boy say so. Knox the night before last at the club, he say to his friend, George Conway and my sister, they going to make a match of it.

[*A horrible change comes over* Daisy's *face as all its features become distorted with rage and jealousy.*]

Daisy. The liar.

[*She stares in front of her, hatred, anger, and mortification seething in her heart. Then she gives a cruel malicious chuckle. She goes quickly to the Korean chest and flings it open. She takes out a parcel of letters and crossing back swiftly to* Lee Tai *thrusts them in his hands.*]

Lee Tai. What is this?

Daisy. They're the letters he wrote me. Let them come into Harry's hands.

Lee Tai. Why?

Daisy. So that Harry may know everything.

Lee Tai. [*After a moment's thought.*] And what will you do for me if I do this for you?

Daisy. What you like…. Only they must get to him quickly. George goes away the day after to-morrow.

Lee Tai. Where is your husband?

Daisy. Kalgan.

Lee Tai. The letters shall reach him to-morrow morning. I'll send them by car.

141

Daisy. It'll be a pleasant surprise for his breakfast.

Lee Tai. Daisy.

Daisy. Go quickly—or I shall change my mind. There'll be plenty of time for everything else after to-morrow.

Lee Tai. I'll go.

[Lee Tai *goes out.* Daisy *gives him a look of contempt.*]

Daisy. Fool.

Amah. What you mean, Daisy?

Daisy. Harry will divorce me. And then....

[Daisy *gives a little cry of triumph.*]

END OF SCENE VI

SCENE VII

The sitting-room in the Andersons' *apartments.*
The scene is the same as Scene iv. Daisy *and the* Amah.
Daisy *is walking restlessly backwards and forwards.*

Daisy. At what time does the train from Kalgan get in?
Amah. Five o'clock, my think so.
Daisy. What time is it now?

[*The* Amah *takes a large gold watch out and looks at it.*]

Amah. My watch no walkee.
Daisy. Why don't you have it mended? What's the good of a watch that doesn't go?
Amah. Gold watch. Eighteen carats. Cost velly much money. Give me plenty face.
Daisy. [*Impatiently.*] Go and ask Wu what time it is.
Amah. I know time. I tell by the sun. More better than European watch. I think half-past four perhaps.
Daisy. Why doesn't George come?
Amah. Perhaps he velly busy.
Daisy. You gave him the note yourself?
Amah. Yes, I give him letter.
Daisy. What did he say?
Amah. He no say nothing. He look: damn, damn.
Daisy. Did you tell him it was very important?
Amah. I say, you come quick. Chop-chop.
Daisy. Yes.
Amah. I tell you before. Why you want me tell you again? He say he come chop-chop when he get away from office.
Daisy. As if the office mattered now. I ought to have gone to him myself.
Amah. You no make him come more quick because you walk up down. Why you no sit still?
Daisy. The train is never punctual. It'll take Harry at least twenty minutes to get out here.
Amah. Lee Tai....
Daisy. [*Interrupting.*] Don't talk to me of Lee Tai. Why on earth should I bother about Lee Tai?
Amah. [*Taking up an opium pipe that is on the table.*] Shall Amah make her little Daisy a pipe? Daisy very restless.

143

Daisy. Have you got opium?

Amah. Lee Tai give me some. [*She shows* Daisy *a small tin box.*] Number one quality. You have one little pipe, Daisy.

Daisy. No.

[Wu *comes in with a card. He gives it to* Daisy.]

Miss Knox. Say I'm not at home.

Wu. Yes, missy.

[*He is about to go out.*]

Daisy. Stop. Is she alone?

Wu. She ride up to gate with gentleman and lady. She say can she see you for two, three minutes.

Daisy. [*After a moment's consideration.*] Tell her to come in.

[Wu *goes out.*]

Amah. What you want to see her for, Daisy?

Daisy. Mind your own business.

Amah. George come very soon now.

Daisy. I shall get rid of her as soon as he does. [*Almost to herself.*] I want to see for myself.

[Sylvia *comes in. She wears a riding-habit.* Daisy *greets her cordially. Her manner, which was restless, becomes on a sudden gay, gracious, and friendly.*]

Daisy. Oh, my dear, how sweet of you to come all this way!

[*The* Amah *slips out.*]

Sylvia. I can only stop a second. I was riding with the Fergusons and we passed your temple. I thought I'd just run in and see how you were. I haven't seen you for an age.

Daisy. Are the Fergusons waiting outside?

Sylvia. They rode on. They said they'd fetch me in five minutes.

Daisy. [*Smiling.*] How did your bridge party go off last night?

Sylvia. How on earth did you hear about that? Did Mr. Conway tell you? I wish you played bridge. We really had rather a lark.

Daisy. George didn't come in till late, I suppose?

144

Sylvia. Oh, no, he got away in fairly decent time. Where there's a will there's a way, you know, even at official functions.

Daisy. [*With a little laugh.*] Oh, I know! I'm expecting him here in a minute. I hope you won't have to go before he comes.

Sylvia. Well, I saw him yesterday. I can live one day without seeing him.

Daisy. I wonder if he can live one day without seeing you?

Sylvia. I'm tolerably sure he can do that.

Daisy. [*As if she were merely teasing.*] A little bird has whispered to me that there's a very pretty blonde in Peking....

Sylvia. [*Interrupting.*] Probably peroxide.

Daisy. Not in this case. Who is not entirely indifferent to the Assistant Chinese Secretary at the British Legation.

Sylvia. Fancy!

Daisy. I suppose you haven't an idea who I'm talking about?

Sylvia. Not a ghost.

Daisy. Then why do you blush to the roots of your hair?

Sylvia. I was outraged at your suggestion that my hair was dyed.

Daisy. It's too bad of me to tease you, isn't it?

Sylvia. I'm a perfect owl. You know what a tactless idiot my brother is. He will chaff me about George Conway, so it makes me self-conscious when anybody talks about him.

Daisy. Darling, it's nothing to be ashamed of. Why shouldn't you be in love with him?

Sylvia. [*With a laugh.*] But I'm not in love with him.

Daisy. Why does your brother chaff you then?

Sylvia. Because he's under the delusion that it's funny.

Daisy. But you do like him, don't you?

Sylvia. Of course I like him.... I think he's a very good sort.

Daisy. Would you marry him if he asked you?

Sylvia. My dear, what are you talking about? The thought never entered my head.

Daisy. Oh, what nonsense! When a man's as attentive to a girl as George has been to you she can't help asking herself if she'd like to marry him or not.

Sylvia. [*Coldly, but still smiling.*] Can't she? I'm afraid I haven't a close acquaintance with that sort of girl.

Daisy. Am I being very vulgar? You know, we half-castes are sometimes.

Sylvia. [*With a trace of impatience.*] Of course you're not vulgar. But I don't know why you want to talk about something that's absolute Greek to me.

Daisy. The natural curiosity of the Eurasian. Everybody tells me that you're engaged to George.

Sylvia. Look at my hand.

[*She stretches out her left hand so that* Daisy *should see there is no ring on the fourth finger.* Daisy *stares at it for a moment.*]

Daisy. You always used to wear an engagement ring.

Sylvia. [*Gravely.*] It was put on my finger by a poor boy who was killed. I meant to wear it always.

Daisy. Why have you taken it off?

[*She looks at* Sylvia. *She can no longer preserve her artificial gaiety and her voice is cold and hard. Before* Sylvia *can answer* George Conway *comes in.*]

Daisy. [*Regaining with an effort her earlier sprightliness.*] There you are at last.

George. I couldn't come sooner. I was with the Minister.

Daisy. We were wondering why you were so late.

Sylvia. Daisy was wondering.

George. [*Shaking hands with Sylvia.*] I thought that was your pony outside.

Sylvia. Clever.

George. The Fergusons were just riding up as I came.

Sylvia. Oh, they've come to fetch me! I must bolt.

George. I'm afraid we kept you up till all sorts of hours last night.

Sylvia. Not a bit. Do I look jaded?

George. Of course not. You young things can stay up till three in the morning and be as fresh as paint. Wait till you're my age.

Sylvia. You haven't passed your hundredth birthday yet, have you?

George. Not quite. But I'm old enough to be your father.

Sylvia. I will not stay and listen to you talk rubbish. Good-bye, Daisy. Do come and see me one day this week.

Daisy. Good-bye.

George. I'll come and help you mount, shall I?

Sylvia. Oh, no, don't bother! Mr. Ferguson is there.

George. Oh, all right!

[*She goes out.*]

Daisy. [*Her smiles vanishing, hostile and cold.*] You might shut the door.

George. [*Doing so.*] I will.

Daisy. Aren't you going to kiss me?

George. Daisy.

Daisy. [*Hastily.*] Oh, no, it doesn't matter! Don't bother.

George. You said you wanted to see me very importantly.

Daisy. It's kind of you to have come.

George. [*With an effort at ease of manner.*] My dear child, what are you talking about? You must know that if there's anything in the world I can do for you I'm only too anxious to do it.

Daisy. Is that girl in love with you?

George. Good heavens, no! What put that idea in your head?

Daisy. The eyes in my head.

George. What perfect nonsense!

Daisy. Has it never occurred to you that she was in love with you?

George. Never.

Daisy. Why do you lie to me? I've been told that you were engaged to her.

George. That's ludicrous. It's absolutely untrue.

Daisy. Yes, I think it is. At the first moment I believed it. And then I thought it over and I knew it couldn't be true. I don't think you'd do anything underhand.

George. At all events I shouldn't do that.

Daisy. In fairness to me or in fairness to her?

George. My dear Daisy, what are you talking about?

Daisy. Did you break with me yesterday so that you might be free to propose to her?

George. No, I swear I didn't.

Daisy. Why are you so emphatic?

George. Oh, Daisy, what's the good of tormenting yourself and tormenting me? You know I loved you just as much as you loved me. But I'm not like you. It was a torture. I knew it was wrong and hateful. I couldn't go on.

Daisy. Do you think it would have seemed wrong and hateful if it hadn't been for Sylvia?

George. Yes.

Daisy. You don't say that very convincingly.

George. I do think it is because she is so loyal, and good and straight that I saw so clearly what a cad I was. I think I found courage to do the only possible thing in her frankness and honesty.

Daisy. I think you deceive yourself. Are you sure this admiration of yours for all her admirable qualities isn't—love?

George. My dear, I'm unfit to love her.

Daisy. She doesn't think so. If you asked her to marry you she'd accept.

George. [*Impatiently.*] What nonsense. What in heaven's name made you think that?

Daisy. I made it my business to find out.

George. Well, you can set your mind at rest. I'm not going to ask her to marry me.

[*The* Amah *comes in.*]

Amah. Five o'clock, Daisy.

Daisy. Leave me alone.

[*The* Amah *goes out.*]

George. When does Harry come back?

Daisy. [*After a pause, in a strange, hoarse voice.*] To-day.

George. [*Surprised at her tone and manner.*] Is anything the matter, Daisy?

Daisy. I'm afraid I have some very bad news for you.

George. [*Startled.*] Oh!

Daisy. You know those letters. I kept them locked in the box. Lee Tai was furious because I wouldn't have anything to do with him. Last night he broke open the box. He's sent the letters to Harry.

George. [*Overwhelmed.*] My God!

Daisy. I'm awfully sorry. It wasn't my fault. I couldn't dream that there was any risk.

George. Was that why you sent for me?

Daisy. Say you don't hate me.

George. Oh, poor Harry!

Daisy. Don't think of him now. Think of me.

George. What do we matter now, you and I? We're a pair of rotters. Harry is a white man through and through. He loved you, and he trusted me.

Daisy. What are we going to do?

George. Give me a minute. I'm all at sixes and sevens. It's such a knock-out blow.

Daisy. Harry will be here soon. His train's due at five.

George. We'll wait for him.

Daisy. What?

George. Did you think I was going to run away? I'll stay and face him.

148

Daisy. He'll kill you.

George. [*With anguish.*] I wish to God he would.

Daisy. Oh, George, how can you be so cruel? Don't you love me any more? I love you. George, what is to become of me if you desert me?

George. Harry loves you so much and he loves me too. Heaven knows what sacrifices he's not capable of. Oh, I'm so ashamed!

Daisy. Why do you bother about him? He doesn't count. He'll get over it. After all, what can he do? He can only divorce me and perhaps we can get him to let me divorce him.

George. Could you *allow* him to do that?

Daisy. It means so little to a man. I don't care, I was thinking of you. It would make it so much easier for you. [*He gives her a quick look. He perceives the allusion to marriage.*] George, George, you wouldn't leave—leave me in the cart.

George. Of course I'll marry you.

Daisy. [*Smiling now, loving and tender.*] Oh, George, we shall be so happy. And you know, some day I'm sure you'll think it's better as it's turned out. I hate all this deceit just as much as you do. Oh, it'll make such a difference when our love can be open and above board. When I'm your wife you'll forget all that has tormented you. Oh, George, I know we shall be happy!

[*All this time* George *has been thinking deeply.*]

George. How do you know that Lee Tai sent those wretched letters to Harry?

Daisy. He sent me a message. He wasn't satisfied with doing a dirty trick. He wanted me to know that he'd done it.

George. How did he know you kept my letters there?

Daisy. I told you I was reading them while I waited for you. He came in and I put them away. I suppose he suspected. It was very easy for him to get into the room after amah and I went away.

George. [*Sarcastically.*] Had you left the key of the box on the table?

Daisy. What do you mean, George? I'd locked it up. Of course I took the key with me. I suppose he broke it open. What does it matter? The harm's done.

George. How do you know Harry received the letters this morning?

Daisy. Lee Tai said he would.

George. In Kalgan?

Daisy. Yes.

George. How did he know Harry was in Kalgan?

149

Daisy. The Chinese know all one's movements.

George. They can't do miracles. Harry was going up there unexpectedly on a private mission. The fellows in that company know very well how to keep their own counsel when it's needful.... I imagine you were the only person in Peking who knew Harry was going to Kalgan.

Daisy. [*Casually.*] Well, it appears I wasn't.

George. How do you suppose Lee Tai found out something that Harry had particularly told you to keep quiet about?

Daisy. How can I tell? He may have found out from the amah for all I know.

George. Surely you hadn't told her?

Daisy. Of course not. She may have read the letter. She always does read my letters.

George. Can she read English?

Daisy. Enough to find out about other people's business.

George. Why should she have told Lee Tai?

Daisy. I suppose he bribed her. She'd do anything for a hundred dollars.

George. Not if it would do you harm.

Daisy. She's not so devoted to me as all that.

George. She's your mother, Daisy.

Daisy. [*Quickly.*] How d'you know?

George. Harry told me.

Daisy. I thought he was too ashamed of it to do that.

George. [*Persistently.*] How did Lee Tai know that Harry was in Kalgan?

Daisy. I tell you I don't know. Why do you cross-examine me? Good God, I'm harassed enough without that! What do you mean?

George. [*He seizes her wrists and draws her violently to him.*] Daisy, did you send those letters to Harry yourself?

Daisy. Never! Do you think I'm crazy?

George. Did you give them to Lee Tai to send?

Daisy. No.

George. God damn you, speak the truth! I will have the truth for once in your life.

[*They stare at one another. He is stern and angry. She pulls herself together. She is fierce and defiant. She shakes herself free of him.*]

Daisy. I gave them to Lee Tai.

George. [*Hiding his face with his hands.*] My God!

Daisy. He told me you were engaged to Sylvia. For a moment I believed it and I gave him the letters. I hardly knew what I was doing. And now, even though I know it wasn't true, I'm glad. I wish I'd done it long before.

George. You fiend!

Daisy. [*Violently.*] Do you think I'm going to let you go so easily? Do you think I've done all I have to let you marry that silly little English girl?

George. [*With anguish.*] Oh, Daisy, how could you?

Daisy. Has it never struck you how you came to be wounded that night? It wasn't you they wanted. It was Harry.

George. I know. [*Suddenly understanding.*] Daisy!

Daisy. Yes, I could do that. I only wish it had succeeded.

George. I can't believe it.

Daisy. You're mine, mine, mine, and I'll never let you go.

George. [*With increasing violence.*] Do you think I can ever look at you again without horror? In my heart I've known always that you were evil. Ten years ago when I first loved you there was a deep instinct within that warned me. Even though my heart was breaking for love of you I knew that you were ruthless and cruel. I've loved you, yes, but all the time I've hated you. I've loved you, but with the baser part of me. All that was in me that was honest and decent and upright revolted against you. Always, always. This love has been a loathsome cancer in my heart. I couldn't rid me of it without killing myself, but I abhorred it. I felt that I was degraded by the love that burned me.

Daisy. What do I care so long as you love? You can think anything you like of me. The fact remains that you love me.

George. If you had no pity for Harry, who raised you from the gutter and gave you everything he had to give, oh, if you'd loved me you'd have had mercy on me. What do you think our life can be together? Don't you know what I shall be? Ruined and abject and hopeless. Oh, not only in the eyes of everyone who knows me shall I be degraded, but in my own. Do you think there's much happiness for you there?

Daisy. I shall have you. That's all the happiness I want. I'd rather be wretched with you—oh, a thousand times—than happy with anyone else.

George. [*Wrathfully, trying to wound her.*] You were tormenting me just now because you were jealous of Sylvia. Do you know what I felt for her? It wasn't love—at least not what you mean by love. I can never love anyone as I've loved you and God knows I'm thankful. But I had such a respect for her. I've been so wretched and she offered me peace. And I did think that some day when all this horror was over, if I could do something to make myself feel clean again, I should go to her and, all unworthy, ask her if she would take me. And now the bitterest pang of all is to think that she must know what an unspeakable cad I've always been.

[*He has flung himself into a chair. He is in despair.* Daisy *goes up to him and going down on her knees beside him puts her arm round him. She is very tender.*]

Daisy. Oh, George, I can make you forget her so easily. You don't know what my love can do. I know I've been horrible, but it's only been because I loved you. Ten years ago I was all that she is. I'm like clay in your hands and you can make me what you will. Oh, George, say you forgive me!

[*In the caressing gestures of her hands as she tries to move him one of them rests by chance on his coat pocket. She feels something hard. He moves slightly away.*]

George. Take care.

Daisy. What's that in your pocket?

George. It's my revolver. Since my accident I've always carried it about with me. It's rather silly, but the Minister asked me to. He said he'd feel safer.

Daisy. Oh, George, if you only knew the agony I suffered when you were brought in! The remorse, the fear! I thought I should go mad.

George. [*With a bitter chuckle.*] It must have been rather a sell for you.

Daisy. Oh, you can laugh! I knew you'd forgive me. My darling.

George. I'm sorry for all the rough things I said to you, Daisy. I don't blame you for anything. You only acted according to your lights. The only person I can blame is myself. It's only reasonable that I should suffer the punishment.

Daisy. My sweetheart!

George. I suppose you know that I shall be quite ruined.

Daisy. You'll have to leave the service. Does that really matter to you very much?

George. It was my whole life.

Daisy. You'll get a job in the post office. With your knowledge of the language they'll simply jump at you. It's a Chinese service. It has nothing to do with Europeans.

George. Do you think the postmaster in a small Chinese city is a very lucrative position?

Daisy. What does money matter? If I'd wanted money I could

have got all I wanted from Lee Tai. We can do with very little. You don't know what a clever housekeeper I am.

George. [*In a level, dead voice.*] I'm sure you're wonderful.

Daisy. We'll go to some city where there are no foreigners. And we shall be together always. We'll have a house high up on the bank and below us the river will flow, flow endlessly.

George. You seem to have got it all mapped out.

Daisy. If you only knew how often I've dreamed of it. Oh, George, I want rest and peace too! I'm so tired. I want endless days to rest in. [*With a puzzled look at him.*] What is the matter? You look so strange.

George. [*With a weary sigh.*] I was thinking of all the things you've been saying to me.

Daisy. If you think it'll be easier for you if you don't marry me, you need not. I don't care anything about that. I'll be your mistress and I'll lie hidden in your house so that no one shall know I'm there. I'll live like a Chinese woman. I'll be your slave and your plaything. I want to get away from all these Europeans. After all, China is the land of my birth and the land of my mother. China is crowding in upon me; I'm sick of these foreign clothes. I have a strange hankering for the ease of the Chinese dress. You've never seen me in it?

George. Never.

Daisy. [*With a smile.*] You'd hardly know me. I'll be a little Chinese girl living in the foreigner's house. Have you ever smoked opium?

George. No. [Daisy *takes the* Amah's *long pipe in her hands.*] Who does that belong to?

Daisy. It's amah's. One day you shall try and I'll make your pipes for you. Lee Tai used to say that no one could make them better than I.

George. However low down the ladder you go there's apparently always a rung lower.

Daisy. After you've smoked a pipe or two your mind grows extraordinarily clear. You have a strange facility of speech and yet no desire to speak. All the puzzles of this puzzling world grow plain to you. You are tranquil and free. Your soul is gently released from the bondage of your body, and it plays, happy and careless, like a child with flowers. Death cannot frighten you, and want and misery are like blue mountains far away. You feel a heavenly power possess you and you can venture all things because suffering cannot touch you. Your spirit has wings and you fly like a bird through the starry wastes of the night. You hold space and time in the hollow of your hand. Then you come upon the dawn, all pearly and gray and silent, and there in the distance, like a dreamless sleep, is the sea.

George. You are showing me a side of you I never knew.

Daisy. Do you think you know me yet? I don't know myself. In my heart there are secrets that are strange even to me, and spells to bind you to me, and enchantments so that you will never weary.

[A pause.]

George. [*Standing up.*] I'll go and get myself a drink. After all these alarums and excursions I really think I deserve it.

Daisy. Amah will bring it to you.

George. Oh, it doesn't matter! I can easily fetch it myself. The whisky's in the dining-room, isn't it?

Daisy. I expect so.

[*He goes out.* Daisy *goes over to a chest which stands in the room and throws it open. She takes out the Manchu dress which Harry once gave her and handles it smilingly. She holds up in both her hands the sumptuous headdress. There is the sound of a door being locked.* Daisy *puts down the headdress and looks at the door enquiringly.*]

Daisy. [*With a little smile.*] What are you locking the door for, George? [*The words are hardly out of her mouth before there is the report of a pistol shot.* Daisy *gives a shriek and rushes towards the door.*] George! George! What have you done? [*She beats frantically on the door.*] Let me in! Let me in! George!

[*The* Amah *comes in running from the courtyard.*]

Amah. What's the matter? I hear shot.

Daisy. Send the boys, quick. We must break down this door.

Amah. I send the boys away. I no want them here when Harry come.

Daisy. George! George! Speak to me. [*She beats violently on the door.*] Oh, what shall I do?

Amah. Daisy, what's the matter?

Daisy. He's killed himself sooner—sooner than....

Amah. [*Aghast.*] Oh!

[Daisy *staggers back into the room.*]

Daisy. Oh, my God!

[*She sinks down on the floor. She beats it with her fist. The* Amah *looks at her for an instant, then with quick determination seizes her shoulder.*]

Amah. Daisy, Harry come soon.

Daisy. [*With a violent gesture.*] Leave me alone. What do I care if Harry comes?

Amah. You no can stay here. Come with me quick.

Daisy. Go away. Damn you!

Amah. [*Stern and decided.*] Don't you talk foolish now. You come. Lee Tai waiting for you.

Daisy. [*With a sudden suspicion.*] Did you know this was going to happen? George! George!

Amah. Harry will kill you if he find you here. Come with me. [*There is a knocking at the outer gate.*] There he is. Daisy! Daisy!

Daisy. Don't torture me.

Amah. I bolt that door. He no get in that way. He must come round through temple. You come quick and I hide you. We slip out when he safe.

Daisy. [*With scornful rage.*] Do you think I'm frightened of Harry?

Amah. He come velly soon now.

[Daisy *raises herself to her feet. A strange look comes over her face.*]

Daisy. Lee Tai has made a mistake again. Bolt that door.

[*The* Amah *runs to it and slips the bolt. While she does this* Daisy *takes the tin of opium and quickly swallows some of the contents. The* Amah *turns round and sees her. She gives a gasp. She runs forward and snatches the tin from* Daisy's *hand.*]

Amah. What you do, Daisy? Daisy, you die!

Daisy. Yes, I die. The day has come. The jungle takes back its own.

Amah. [*Distraught.*] Oh, Daisy! Daisy! My little flower.

Daisy. How long will it take? [*The* Amah *sobs desperately.* Daisy *goes to the Manchu clothes and takes them up.*] Help me to put these on.

Amah. [*Dumbfounded.*] What you mean, Daisy?

Daisy. Curse you, do as I tell you!

Amah. I think you crazy. [Daisy *slips into the long skirt and the* Amah *with trembling hands helps her into the coat. In the middle of her dressing* Daisy *staggers.*] Daisy.

Daisy. [*Recovering herself.*] Don't be a fool. I'm all right.
Amah. [*In a terrified whisper.*] There's Harry.
Daisy. Give me the headdress.
Harry. [*Outside.*] Open the door.
Daisy. Be quick.
Amah. I no understand. You die, Daisy. You die.

[*The knocking is repeated more violently.*]

Harry. [*Shouting.*] Daisy! Amah! Open the door. If you don't open I'll break it down.

[Daisy *is ready. She steps on to the pallet and sits in the Chinese fashion.*]

Daisy. Go to the door. Open when I tell you.

[*There is by* Daisy's *side a box in which are the paints and pencils the Chinese lady uses to make up her face.* Daisy *opens it. She takes out a hand mirror.*]

Harry. Who's there? Open, I tell you! Open!

[Daisy *puts rouge on her cheeks. She takes a black pencil and touches her eyebrows. She gives them a slight slant so that she looks on a sudden absolutely Chinese.*]

Daisy. Open!

[*The Amah draws the bolt and* Harry *bursts in.*]

Harry. Daisy! [*He comes forward impetuously and then on a sudden stops. He is taken aback. Something, he knows not what, comes over him and he feels helpless and strangely weak.*] Daisy, what does it mean? These letters. [*He takes them out of his pocket and thrusts them towards her. She takes no notice of him.*] Daisy, speak to me. I don't understand. [*He staggers towards her with outstretched hands.*] For God's sake, say it isn't true.

[*Motionless she contemplates in the mirror the Chinese woman of the reflection.*]

THE END